# "I Wish I Had A Sister,"

Susannah said wistfully. "Can you and Mommy get one for me?"

Mara exchanged a horrified look with Falcon, whose lips twisted in a wry smile.

"That's entirely up to your mother," he said.

"Will you, Mommy?"

"It's not quite as simple as getting you that pony you want," Mara said as she sent a cutting glance toward Falcon. "Why don't we wait a while, until you're well? Then we'll see."

Mara saw Falcon's eyebrow arch, but she refused to take away any of Susannah's dreams, no matter how farfetched. Especially since there was no telling how much longer Susannah had to dream dreams.

Dear Reader,

Welcome once again to Silhouette Desire! Enter into a world of powerful love and sensuous romance, a world where your most passionate fantasies come true.

September begins with a sexy, sassy MAN OF THE MONTH, *Family Feud* by Barbara Boswell, a writer you've clearly indicated is one of your favorites.

And just as exciting—if you loved Joan Johnston's fantastic HAWK'S WAY series, then don't miss CHILDREN OF HAWK'S WAY, beginning with *The Unforgiving Bride*.

The month is completed with stories from Lass Small, Karen Leabo, Beverly Barton and Carla Cassidy. *Next* month, look for a MAN OF THE MONTH by Annette Broadrick *and* the continuation of Joan Hohl's BIG, BAD WOLFE series.

So, relax, read, enjoy…and fall in love all over again with Silhouette Desire.

Sincerely yours,

Lucia Macro
Senior Editor

Please address questions and book requests to:
Silhouette Reader Service
U.S.: 3010 Walden Ave., P.O. Box 1325, Buffalo, NY 14269
Canadian: P.O. Box 609, Fort Erie, Ont. L2A 5X3

# JOAN JOHNSTON
# THE UNFORGIVING BRIDE

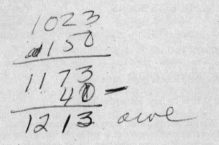

```
 1023
  150
─────
 1173
   40 ─
─────
 1213  owe
```

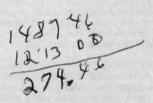

```
 148744
 1213 0D
─────
 274.46
```

**SILHOUETTE** *Desire®*
Published by Silhouette Books
America's Publisher of Contemporary Romance

SILHOUETTE BOOKS

ISBN 0-373-05878-0

THE UNFORGIVING BRIDE

**Printed in U.S.A.**

## JOAN JOHNSTON

started reading romances to escape the stress of being an attorney with a major national law firm. She soon discovered that writing romances was a lot more fun than writing legal bond indentures. Since then, she has published a number of historical and contemporary category romances. In addition to being an author, Joan is the mother of two children. In her spare time, she enjoys sailing, horseback riding and camping.

This book is dedicated to all
single mothers who face disasters—
large and small—
and find a way to survive.

## ACKNOWLEDGMENTS
I would like to thank St. Jude Children's Research
Hospital in Memphis, Tennessee, for providing me
with up-to-date information about the symptoms and
treatment of acute lymphocytic leukemia and for
answering all my questions willingly and cheerfully.
I'm afraid I represented the sick little girl in my book
so humanly to their representative that I was asked,
"Does your daughter have this disease?"
Thankfully, she does not.

I have taken some liberty in representing the material
given to me, but the symptoms, treatment and survival
statistics for this disease are accurately stated.

# Prologue

**F**alcon noticed the woman right away, even though she was standing in the middle of a crowded sidewalk in downtown Dallas. She was not the sort of female who usually attracted his attention, being boyishly slim and merely pretty, rather than beautiful. But there was something about her that drew his eyes and held him spellbound.

He had barely begun to admire her assets—long, silky black hair whipped by the hot summer breeze, spectacular blue eyes and a tall, supple body—when he spotted the little girl at her side. The woman was joined a moment later by a man who slipped his arm around her slender waist and captured her mouth in a hard, possessive kiss. The little girl quickly claimed the man's attention, and he leaned down to listen to her excited chatter.

Falcon felt a sharp stab of envy that he wasn't the man in the quaint family picture. Not that he wanted kids, or wanted to be married, for that matter, but he would have given anything to be on the receiving end of the warm, approving look the woman gave the man as he attended to the little girl.

He was startled to realize that he knew the man. Which meant he could easily wrangle an introduction to the woman.

*She's married.*

Falcon didn't dally with married women. At least, he never had in the past. He pursed his lips thoughtfully. There was no reason why he couldn't meet her. Without stopping to think, he approached the trio.

"Grant? Grant Ainsworth?" Falcon inquired, though he knew he wasn't mistaken.

"Falcon Whitelaw!" the man exclaimed. "I haven't seen you in—it must be ten years!"

"Nearly that. Guess we lost touch after graduation from Tech," Falcon said with a smile as he extended his hand to meet the one that had been thrust at him. He forced himself to keep his eyes on his old football teammate from Texas Tech. But he wanted to meet the woman. He wanted to feast his eyes on her face at close range. He wanted to figure out what it was that made her so alluring.

"What have you been doing with yourself, Grant?" Falcon asked.

"Got married," Grant replied with a smug grin. "This is my wife, Mara, and my daughter, Susannah."

Falcon turned to greet Mara Ainsworth. He was sorry she wasn't one of those progressive women who shook hands with a man. He would have liked to touch her. She nodded her head and smiled at him, and he felt his stomach do a queer turn. He lifted a finger to his Stetson in acknowledgement of her. "Ma'am."

Because he knew it was expected of him, he lowered his eyes to the little girl. She was hiding half behind her mother's full skirt. Susannah had Mara's black hair, but her eyes were hazel, rather than blue. "Howdy," he said. "You're a pretty little miss. Almost as pretty as your mother."

The little girl giggled and hid her face completely.

From the corner of his eye, Falcon caught the flush of pleasure on Mara's face. He wanted to touch her cheek, to feel the heat beneath the skin.

"How old is your daughter?" he asked Mara. He needed a reason to look at her. His eyes lingered, cataloging each exquisite feature.

"Susannah's seven," Mara replied.

Falcon heard Grant talking, but he couldn't take his eyes off Mara. For a moment he thought he saw something in her open gaze, an attraction to him as strong as the one he felt for her. But he knew that was only wishful thinking.

Her lids lowered demurely so her lashes created two coal crescents on milky white skin. Whatever she was feeling, it was hidden from him now. Her lips parted slightly, and he could just see the edges of her teeth. He had to restrain a harsh intake of breath at the overpowering desire he felt to claim her mouth with his. He had never felt a need so strong or so demanding.

Falcon was aware that Grant was asking him something, but he only caught the last half of the sentence.

"...so if you're staying the night in Dallas, maybe we could get together and have a few drinks for old times' sake," Grant finished.

Falcon saw the quick flash of annoyance on Mara's face. Obviously she would rather have Grant to herself than share him with an old friend. Falcon started to give her what she wanted but realized that if he had a few drinks with Grant he could find out more about Mara, more about the state of their marriage. It looked happy from the outside, but if there were problems, maybe there was a chance Mara would welcome his attention.

Falcon hated what he was thinking. It wasn't like him to go after some other man's woman. But there was something about Mara Ainsworth that struck a chord deep inside him. If he had found her unattached, he might even have contemplated giving up his bachelor freedom. But it was folly to let himself even think about her so long as she was another man's wife.

By the time Falcon had come to the conclusion he ought to just get the hell away from the Ainsworths, he realized he had already invited Grant to have drinks with him at a bar near the stockyards.

"What brings you to town, anyway?" Grant asked.

"I'm here to buy cattle for my ranch."

"Didn't know you had a ranch of your own," Grant said.

"I inherited the B-Bar from my grandfather, my mother's father, about five years ago," Falcon replied.

Grant whistled in appreciation. "If I remember rightly, that's quite a spread."

Falcon hadn't done anything to earn the B-Bar, but he was proud of owning it. It *was* a big spread. He glanced at Mara to see if she was impressed. Most women were. But she was watching Grant. She had caught her lower lip with her teeth and was chewing on it. She looked worried about something. Was his rendezvous with Grant going to interrupt some previously made plans?

Falcon had grown up in a family where strong wills were the norm. He had learned that with determination and a little charm, he could usually get what he wanted. As a result, he wasn't used to denying himself anything. That had worked out fine, because there hadn't been anyone but himself to please for the past five years since he had inherited his grandfather's ranch. Suddenly he found himself wanting to take the worry from Mara's brow, even if it meant giving up the opportunity to quiz Grant about her while they were having drinks.

"Look," Falcon said, "if you all have other plans for the evening, I don't want to intrude."

Mara had opened her mouth to respond when Grant said, "No plans. I'll meet you at eight. See you then."

Falcon watched the gentle sway of Mara's hips as Grant led her away. She glanced back at Falcon over her shoulder and caught him staring at her. He felt himself flush, something he couldn't remember doing for a long, long time. He tipped his Stetson to her one more time. It looked like she wanted to say something to him, but Grant kept walking, his arm around her, and the moment was lost.

When the three of them were gone from sight, Falcon exhaled a long, loud sigh of regret. The woman of his dreams had just walked out of his life. He debated whether he ought to do something else tonight and leave a message at the bar for Grant that he couldn't make it. His feelings for Mara Ainsworth were dangerous. If he pursued the matter, he was asking for trouble.

But when eight o'clock came, Falcon was waiting at the Longhorn Bar. Five minutes later, Grant Ainsworth came in. There was a bond between teammates that extended beyond ordinary friendship, and Falcon was reminded of all the times he and Grant had tipped a brew after winning a difficult football game. He knew nothing of what had happened to Grant after college, but he intended to find out.

A country band with a wailing violin was playing up front near the dance floor, but Falcon had settled in one of the booths near the back, where the noise wasn't quite so loud nor the smoke so bad.

"What are you drinking?" he asked as Grant slid in across from him.

"I'll have a whiskey, neat," Grant replied.

Falcon gestured to a waitress wearing skintight jeans and a peasant blouse and ordered the drink Grant had asked for and another Pearl beer for himself.

When the drinks arrived, Grant held up his glass and said, "To pretty women."

Falcon grinned. "I'll drink to that." He took a sip of beer; Grant had finished his whiskey in a few swallows.

Grant slammed his glass onto the table and said, "That went down pretty damn smooth. I think I'll have another." Grant gestured and had the waitress bring him another whiskey.

"You need any ranch hands for that place of yours?" Grant asked after he had taken a sip of the second drink.

Falcon was startled by the question. "You need work?"

Grant shrugged. "Been laid off recently. Could use work if you've got it."

Actually, Falcon was sure he had all the help he needed. But he thought of Mara and Susannah without food on the table and said, "Sure. There's always room for another hand."

Grant's shoulders visibly relaxed. He finished off the second whiskey and called for another. "You don't know what a relief that is. Mara was beginning to think I would never... But I've got a job, after all, so everything will be fine."

It was plain from the look on Grant's face that he and his wife must have argued over the matter. Falcon was happy to change the subject to what he wanted to talk about most.

"Where did you meet Mara?"

"Her father was foreman on a ranch in west Texas where I worked right after college. I took one look at her and knew she was the one for me. It took a little convincing to get her to say yes. But she did. We've been married for eight years now."

"Where have you been living?"

Grant looked sheepish. "Here and there around Texas. We've moved every year or so. Last job I had was in Victoria. We came to Dallas because I heard some ranches around here were hiring help."

Falcon frowned. Most cowhands were footloose and fancy free—when they were single. A married man settled down in one place and raised his family. He wondered whether Grant had willingly left all those jobs, or whether there was something he had done to get himself fired. He had seemed steady enough in college, but college was ten years ago.

Had Grant Ainsworth become a thief? Was he a bully? Lazy? Incompetent? Cantankerous? Any of those faults would get him laid off in a hurry.

What had it been like for Mara to move around like that? Could she be happy with a man who was constantly losing his job? He recalled the adoring look on Mara's face when she had watched Grant with Susannah. Whatever Grant's shortcomings, Mara apparently still loved him.

"There are some houses on the property for hired hands. You're welcome to use one of them," he heard himself offer.

"I'd appreciate that," Grant said. Only he wasn't looking at Falcon when he answered.

Falcon was amazed and appalled when he realized that Grant was flirting with a pair of women sitting at a table across from them. He felt outraged on Mara's behalf. A man with a wife like her waiting for him at home had no business making eyes at other women. Suddenly Falcon didn't want to be where he was anymore.

"Look, I've got to be up early tomorrow. The drinks are on me—for old times' sake. I'll see you when you get to the ranch." Falcon threw a twenty on the table.

"There's no need—"

Falcon cut Grant off with a quick shake of his head. "Call it a celebration of your new job."

At the door to the bar Falcon glanced back and saw that the two women had already joined Grant in the booth. He scowled. Sonofabitch was cheating on his wife! Falcon felt a burning anger deep in his gut.

Falcon realized he just might have discovered why Grant had been let go from jobs so often. Suppose Grant played around with women wherever he went? That would certainly raise the hackles of the men he worked with and get him booted fast. Falcon grimaced. What kind of man had he just hired to work on the B-Bar?

Falcon thought of having Mara Ainsworth living on the B-Bar, in a house where he could see her every day. Knowing her husband didn't appreciate her. Knowing she loved the bastard anyway.

It was going to be hell.

Falcon had wanted to see Mara Ainsworth again, but he had never dreamed it would be at her husband's funeral. He stood at the back of a crowd of mourners shrouded in black, waiting for a chance to speak to her, to tell her how sorry he was that Grant was dead. And he was sorry, for Grant's sake. No one deserved to die that young. Deep down, in places where honesty reigned, he felt that Mara was better off without him. But he wasn't going to voice those feelings. He owed Grant that, at least.

But he couldn't forgive Grant for the utter senselessness of his death: his friend had been killed in a one-car accident the same night Falcon had met him in the Longhorn Bar. Falcon bitterly regretted leaving Grant with money for several more drinks. Obviously Grant hadn't sobered up before he got behind the wheel. It was a tragedy that happened all too often, and Falcon could only be grateful that there had been no innocent victims in the accident.

If Falcon felt guilty at all, it was because he coveted Grant's widow. Mara was free now. He could have her if he wanted her—after a decent period of mourning, of course. Even he wasn't blackguard enough to go after a grieving widow.

But he wanted her. More than he ever had.

Dressed in black, Mara had an ethereal beauty. The deep circles under her eyes only made her look more hauntingly attractive. He knew she couldn't have gotten much sleep in the past week since Grant's death. Susannah stood beside her mother looking bewildered.

Falcon had tried to see Mara when he first heard about the accident, but realized he didn't know how to find her. He had read an announcement of the funeral services and made plans to attend. That way he could talk to her and extend his sympathy. And find out where she planned to go from here.

Because he wanted to know where he could find her when she had finished mourning Grant Ainsworth.

The grave-side service had ended, and most of those gathered for the funeral had returned to their cars. Susannah had apparently gone with one of Mara's friends, because Mara was alone beside Grant's grave when Falcon approached her.

"Mara," he said.

It took her eyes a second to focus, but he knew the instant she recognized him, because her features twisted with loathing.

"How dare you show your face here!" she said in a harsh, bitter voice. "My husband is dead, and it's all your fault!"

Falcon was stunned at her accusation.

"You invited him to that bar! You got him drunk! And then you let him drive home!"

"I—"

"I hate you!" she said in a venomous voice. "I hope you rot in hell! I hope someone you loves dies a horrible death!"

She opened her mouth to speak, but all that came out was a low, ululating cry of pain. Her face crumpled in a mask of despair as she dropped to the grass beside her husband's newly dug grave. Her body shook with sobs of grief.

There was thickness in Falcon's throat that made it painful to swallow. He had never dreamed that she would blame him. How could she think he was responsible? He hadn't even been there when Grant left the bar. It wasn't his fault. She was wrong.

Not even in the farthest reaches of his mind had he planned to get Grant drunk and send him out to die in a fiery one-car crash. He had wanted Mara, it was true. But he had never wished Grant dead so that he could have her.

Small chance of his having her now. She hated his guts. She never wanted to see him again. She would as soon scratch out his eyes as look at him.

Falcon wanted to reach out to comfort her, to hold her in his arms and let her cry out her pain against his chest. He actually went so far as to touch her shoulder. "If there's ever anything I can do to help..."

The instant she realized who had touched her, she turned on him. He had never seen a woman's face contort in such fury and revulsion.

"Get away from me!" she hissed. "I don't need your kind of help. Go to hell, or go anywhere at all, but don't ever come near me again!"

He had backed away, stumbled over something, then turned and fled. He felt as though a tight band was constricting his chest. He couldn't breathe. He couldn't swallow. He felt like crying.

It was over. Mara was gone from his life before she had ever been a part of it. She hated him. She blamed him for Grant's death. He would never see her again.

But it would be a long time before he forgot the look of loathing toward him on Mara Ainsworth's face.

# One

---

*One year later*

Mara had tried every other alternative, and there was only one left. She had to swallow her pride and approach Falcon Whitelaw for the help he had once offered. Although, she couldn't imagine him even giving her a chance to open her mouth before he shut the door in her face. Mara shuddered when she remembered the awful things she had said to him, even if they were true.

But Susannah was sick, very sick, and she needed treatment that would cost thousands of dollars. Mara had applied to a number of agencies for help,

and it was available, but only if she and Susannah
left home and traveled to another state. Life was
grim enough these days without leaving behind everything that was familiar.

On Grant's death, Mara had used most of his life
insurance to buy a home for herself and Susannah.
She had vowed never to move again. If there was
any way to stay in Dallas, where they had finally
grown roots—shallow ones, but roots, nevertheless—Mara intended to pursue it. She had exhausted every other road to achieve her goal. There
was only one left. She had to approach Falcon
Whitelaw and ask him for money to help with Susannah's medical expenses.

Begging left a bitter taste in her mouth. But Mara
was willing to humble herself in any way that was
necessary to make sure Susannah got the treatment
she needed. It was galling to have to approach the
one man in the world she blamed for her current
predicament. If Grant hadn't died in that accident,
they would have had the health insurance he usually received as a part of his compensation. But
Grant had been between jobs, so there was nothing. Instead Mara had been caught in every mother's nightmare. She had a sick child and no
insurance to pay for medical bills.

Health insurance had been the last thing on her
mind when Grant had left her widowed, and she
found herself unemployed with a meager amount of
life insurance and a child to raise. She had used the

balance of the life insurance left after she bought the house to pay college tuition, believing that an education was the best investment for their future. It was a wise move, but had left the two of them exposed to the disaster that had occurred.

Mara hadn't even realized, at first, that Susannah was sick. In the months following Grant's death, her daughter had been tired and listless and seemed uninterested in doing the things she normally did. Mara had thought Susannah was merely grieving in her own way. Until one day Susannah didn't get out of bed at all. She had a high fever, and nothing Mara did could bring it down.

She took Susannah to the emergency room of the hospital and experienced the horror of watching her small, helpless child be hooked up to dozens of tubes and monitors. The diagnosis of Susannah's illness had come as a shock. Mara had sat stunned in the chair before Dr. Sortino's cluttered desk and listened with disbelief.

*Acute lymphocytic leukemia.*

"Children die of that," Mara had managed to gasp.

A pair of sympathetic brown eyes had looked out from Dr. Sortino's gaunt face. "Not as many as in the past. Nearly three-quarters of all children diagnosed with this disease today live."

"What about the rest?" Mara asked. "What about Susannah?"

"Our cure rate with chemotherapy is ninety percent. If that doesn't work, there's always a bone-
marrow transplant to consider."

Mara had stared at him with unseeing eyes. *Chemotherapy*. She had never known anyone person-
ally who had taken chemotherapy. But she had read
enough, and seen enough on television, to know that
chemotherapy made you vomit, and that your hair
fell out. The thought of that happening to her precious daughter, the thought of all Susannah's long
black hair falling out, made her feel faint.

"Mrs. Ainsworth? Are you all right?"

Dr. Sortino was on one knee beside her, keeping
her from sliding out of the chair. She felt the sting
of tears in her nose and eyes. "No, I'm not all
right!" She fixed a blazing stare on the doctor who
had been the messenger of such ill tidings.

"I'm angry," she spat. "I'm furious, in fact!
Why Susannah? How did this happen? She's just a
little girl. *She's only eight years old!*"

Dr. Sortino's eyes were no longer sympathetic. A
look of pain and resignation had glazed his eyes after her vituperative attack. He rose and returned to
his place behind the desk, putting a physical barrier
between them that did little to protect him from her
anger and despair.

"I'm sorry, Mrs. Ainsworth," he said. "There are
as many as a dozen factors that may have been responsible for Susannah contracting the disease. We
haven't done enough tests yet to make a guess on the

precise reasons for her illness. But we can cure it…in most cases. You're lucky. Susannah has a tremendous chance of survival. With other diseases…"

He left her to contemplate her good fortune. But Mara didn't feel lucky. Leukemia was a serious disease. Her precious, wonderful daughter might die. "When do you start treatment?" she asked. "Will Susannah have to stay in the hospital? How will we know if it works?"

That was when kindly Dr. Sortino had started asking questions about insurance. That was when she had realized the enormity of the cost of treatment, and the hospital's inability to absorb another patient of this kind without a payment from some source.

"There are other facilities that can serve your needs better if you can't pay at least a portion of the costs up front," the doctor had said.

But those facilities were in another state.

Mara had tried buying insurance, but Susannah's illness was a preexisting condition and could not be covered.

"But I don't need insurance for anything else!" she had argued.

After the insurance companies turned a deaf ear, Mara tried the various foundations that provided assistance for children. And got the same answer. Help was available only if she was willing to go somewhere else to get it.

Mara knew she was foolish for clinging to the familiar, but she wasn't sure she could survive weeks, and maybe months, of living in a Ronald McDonald House in a strange city, all alone with only Susannah and her fears to keep her company. She needed a place that was home. She needed the support of the few friends she had made. And Susannah needed the normalcy of school and friends around her during her recuperation.

Her daughter was going to be one of the lucky seventy-three percent who were cured of the disease. Mara refused to consider any other outcome to Susannah's treatment.

But she needed money and needed it fast. Borrowing was out of the question. She had just finished her first year of college, working part-time as a cook in one of the college hangouts. She didn't qualify for the sizable loan she needed without some security, and she hadn't enough equity in the house to do the job.

On the other hand, Grant had told her before he'd gone to the bar that Falcon Whitelaw was as rich as Croesus, that he had inherited a fortune from his maternal grandfather, including the B-Bar Ranch on the outskirts of Dallas. Falcon wouldn't even miss the thousands of dollars it was going to cost for Susannah's care. Besides, she was going to offer him something in return.

Mara had grown up at her mother's side and knew everything there was to know about keeping house for a rancher. She planned to trade her services as housekeeper to Falcon in exchange for his financial assistance in paying Susannah's medical bills. She feared she would end up indentured to him for a long time. Just the initial treatment was going to cost nearly $25,000.

Which reasoning all led her to the front doorstep of Falcon Whitelaw's B-Bar Ranch. She had to admit the ranch wasn't what she had expected. The terrain was flat and grassy, but long ago someone had planted live oaks around the house. It had the look of a Spanish hacienda, with its red tile roof and thick, whitewashed adobe walls.

Her hand was poised to knock, her heart in her throat. She swallowed both heart and pride and rapped her knuckles on the arched, heavy oak panel.

No one answered.

She knocked harder, longer and louder.

At last, the door opened.

Falcon had been out late carousing, and he had just dragged on a pair of jeans to answer the door, not even bothering to button them all the way up. They hung down on his hipbones and revealed his white briefs in the vee at the top. He scratched his belly and put one bare foot atop the other. He squinted, his eyes unable to focus in the harsh sunlight that was streaming in through the crack he had opened in the door. He thought better of trying to see and put a hand over his eyes, pressing his temples with forefinger and thumb in an attempt to stop the pounding inside his head.

"Who's there?" he muttered.

Mara stared in disbelief at the bleary-eyed, tousle-headed, unshaved face that had appeared at the door. "It's eleven o'clock," she said with asperity. "Are you just getting up?"

"Good God," Falcon said with a moan. He would never forget that condemning voice, not in a million years. Of all the days for her to show up at the B-Bar, she had to come now. He slowly lowered his hand and squinted painfully into the sunlight until his eyes had adjusted enough to confirm what his ears had told him.

It was Mara Ainsworth, all right. She was wearing that same derisive, accusing look she had worn at Grant's funeral.

Falcon considered shutting the door in her face. He didn't owe her anything. He had offered her his help a year ago, and she had refused it in no uncertain terms.

*So what is she doing here now?*

From the look on her face she had come to play Puritan temperance woman. He just wasn't up for the game.

Mara's belief that Falcon was an irresponsible care-for-nobody was reaffirmed as she eyed him from head to barefoot toes. Her nose wrinkled in disgust when the smell of beer assaulted her nostrils. He was drunk! Or rather, had been. He looked hung over at the moment.

"Are you going to invite me inside?" she demanded.

Falcon was a second late responding, and Mara invited herself in, since he was obviously in no condition to do it. She pushed past Falcon and walked through the arched doorway right into the living room, leaving him standing at the open door.

The house was dark and cool. The furniture was leather and wood, large and heavy, the sort of thing the conquistadors must have brought with them from Spain. Navajo rugs were thrown on the red brick floor, and Mara found herself facing shelves full of Hopi Indian decorations. Arches inset along the walls held ornamental vases, adding to the Spanish flavor of the room. It was beautiful. It felt like a home. Which was odd, she thought, considering a bachelor lived here.

Without turning to face Falcon she said, "I need to talk to you." Mara surreptitiously rubbed her stomach where she had brushed against him. Her belly was doing strange things. He was an animal—that was why she felt this animal magnetism toward him. She hated the man. It was absolutely ridiculous to think she could be attracted to him.

She turned to face him, willing herself not to feel anything.

But she hadn't forgotten the powerful shudders that had rippled through her when Falcon looked at her the first time they had met. Something had definitely happened that hot summer day on the street in Dallas. She despised herself for what she had felt then. And it had happened again just now.

*Animal magnetism,* she repeated to herself. *That's all it is.*

Falcon shut the door with a quiet click and leaned back against it. He folded his arms across his bare chest, crossed one bare ankle over the other and stared at her. "I didn't think you ever wanted to see me again."

She flushed. The color started at the edge of her square-necked blouse and shot right up her throat to her cheeks, where it sat in two bright pink spots. "I...I didn't."

His eyes narrowed. "But now you do?"

She swallowed hard and nodded once.

"Well." He paused. "Well." Falcon didn't know what else to say. This was certainly an astounding turn of events. Just when he had convinced himself he could live without her, the woman of his dreams had shown up at his door. Of course, she hadn't exactly picked a moment when he was at his best.

Falcon didn't ask her to sit. He didn't want her to be any more comfortable than he was. And he was downright miserable.

That didn't keep him from feeling the singular, consuming attraction for her that had struck him the first moment he saw her. And this time he knew he wasn't mistaken—she was feeling it, too. His lips curved in a self-satisfied smile. So, she was ready to admit the attraction she felt and had come to apologize for all those horrible things she had said to him.

Falcon gave free rein to the fierce sexual desire he felt for Mara Ainsworth. His groin tightened, and his blood began to hum. He refused to hide his arousal. Since she had invited herself in, she could just put up with the condition she found him in.

Mara was appalled at the blatant sensuality in Falcon's heavy-lidded stare. There was no hiding the bulge that was lovingly cupped by his butter-soft jeans. Even more appalling was her body's reaction to the prickly situation in which she found herself. She was dumbfounded by her gut response to Falcon's maleness. Her breasts felt heavy, and her belly tensed with expectation.

It was time to state her business and get out.

"I've come to get the help you offered a year ago. I need money. Lots of it."

Mara saw the shock on Falcon's face and hurried to finish before he could throw her out. "Susannah is very ill. She could die." She swallowed over the lump of pain that always arose when she said those words. "She has leukemia."

Falcon had dropped his lazy pose against the door and was standing now on both feet with his hands balled at his sides.

"When Grant died he was between jobs and we didn't have any insurance and I don't have the money for chemotherapy and I've tried to get it other places but they want us to leave Dallas and Grant said you have lots of money so you wouldn't miss it and I think it would be better for both Susannah and me if we stayed where we are. So can you help us?"

Falcon had taken several steps toward Mara during this breathless speech. As he reached out to give her the comfort she so obviously needed, she took a step back away from him.

So. She wanted his money, but she didn't want him. That was blatantly clear.

"I'll work for you," she choked out. "I'll keep house, cook, clean, whatever you need. I know how to keep ranch books. I'll pay you back in service for every penny, I promise you that. I'm... I'm desperate. Please."

Falcon felt sick to his stomach. Mara, pretty Mara, had been reduced to begging. And she wasn't even asking him to give her the money. She was going to pay it all back. She didn't want to be beholden to him. Because she despised him.

It was there on her face every time she looked at him. She still blamed him for Grant's death. She was never going to forgive him.

So why should he give her the money?

*Because there is a chance, just the slightest one, but a chance, that you might be responsible in part for her predicament.* Falcon was shaken to the core by that possibility.

And that poor kid. He remembered Susannah's hazel eyes peeping out from behind Mara's skirt on the day he met her and the childish giggle before she hid herself completely from his sight. It was a shame for any kid to be sick, but it caught him in the gut to imagine that engaging little girl bedridden.

"Is Susannah . . . will she get well?" he asked.

"There's a good chance, a three-to-one chance, she'll be cured by the chemotherapy. But the hospital won't start treatments before I assure them I can pay. Can you . . . will you help?"

"Give me a figure. I'll see my accountant tomorrow and cut you a check."

"Thank you," Mara said.

He watched her take a step toward him, as though to hug him, to share the joy and relief she was feeling. Then she must have remembered who he was, because she stiffened and stopped herself.

"Thank you," she said again.

But she didn't look at him. She was looking at her hands, which were threaded together and clenched so hard her knuckles were white.

"I can start work right away," she said.

"That won't be necessary," he said in a harsh voice.

Her head snapped up, and her brow furrowed. "I don't understand."

"I'd go nuts with you stomping around here all self-righteous, watching every little move I make and raking me over the coals with those big blue eyes of yours. Thanks, but no thanks. You can have the money, but I'll dispense with your services, if it's all the same to you."

Mara was stung by the image he had painted of her. She wanted to fling his money back in his face, but she had to think of Susannah. She bit her lower lip hard and kept her peace.

"Are we finished with this talk?" Falcon asked irritably. "Because I have a headache, and I'd like to get some aspirin."

"I'll pay you back," Mara said quietly. "Somehow." She hurried to the door. It meant going past Falcon. He didn't move to get out of her way, and she shivered as their bodies brushed.

"Aw, hell. You're not going to get cooties if we touch."

"I didn't—I only—" she stuttered.

"Just get the hell out of here," he said in disgust. He opened the door and held it as she rushed through, dropping a slip of paper in his hand with a breathless "My address," and then slammed it behind her.

"Women! Who the hell needs them!"

He crumpled the paper without looking at it and tossed it on the floor. He wouldn't see her to give her the check. He would have his accountant do it. There was no question, though, about his helping her. He owed it to Grant, and to the little girl who was sick. He owed Mara nothing. He hoped their paths never crossed again.

Finally, at last, he and Mara Ainsworth were quits.

# Two

---

"You don't have the money."

"What?"

"You heard me, Falcon. I said you don't have the money to be giving a blank check to some bimbo."

"Watch what you say, Aaron. Mara Ainsworth is a lady."

"My apologies. That doesn't change your situation."

"Just what, exactly, is my situation?" Falcon asked.

"To be blunt, you've damn near run through your grandfather's fortune in the past five years."

Falcon was stunned. He stopped pacing the thick carpet in his accountant's high-rise Dallas office and sank into a leather-and-chrome chair. "You're kidding, right?"

"I wish I were," Aaron said.

"Why didn't you say something sooner?" he demanded.

"I did."

Falcon remembered a conversation or two when Aaron had warned him not to make some high-risk investments. Then there were the cars. And the parties. The trips to Europe. The fancy studs and champion bulls. And the gifts he had given to his lady friends. He hadn't thought it was possible to spend a fortune in just five years.

"How much have I got left?" he asked, still a little stunned by Aaron's news.

"Enough to keep the B-Bar afloat—if you're careful and give the ranch some attention. Not enough to be loaning thousands of dollars to some woman."

"Lady," Falcon insisted. "Mara is a lady."

"Lady," Aaron conceded.

Falcon dropped his head into his hands. He could always go to his family for help; his parents and his brother and sister had assets if he really needed a loan to help Mara. And he had two uncles and an aunt. But he would be too ashamed to admit to any of them that he had squandered his inheritance. He would never live down the humiliation. And he couldn't bear to see the look on his father's face if he disappointed him. His mother would hide the pain she felt at his failure, because she knew how hard his father could be on anyone who threatened her happiness—even, or especially, her children.

Falcon was the middle child of the Three White-law Brats, as they had come to be known in the vicinity around Hawk's Way, the northwest Texas ranch where he had been raised. Falcon's father, Garth, had been a hard taskmaster, demanding honesty and responsibility and accomplishment from his two sons and daughter. But Garth White-law had held the leash too tight, and all three of them—his elder brother, Zachary, and his younger sister, Callen and himself—had revolted.

They had formed a secret alliance, the Fearless Threesome, and protected each other, deftly covering one another's tracks when they were caught out in some prank. Not that they had been vicious or mean in what they had done, but they had been incorrigible, unmanageable, all three of them, daring anything and often finding themselves in desperate situations that required feats of bravado to escape.

They had been punished for their recklessness, but had remained undaunted. As a child, Falcon's behavior had been as wild and untamed as his Comanche forbearers. He hadn't improved much over the years. At thirty, he was a maverick who refused to be tied down to anything or anyone.

His siblings weren't much more settled. His sister, Callen, was a black-haired, brown-eyed rebel who had defied their father's attempts to direct her life by twice accepting marriage proposals against his wishes—and breaking both engagements when the man turned out to be the cad her father had told her he was. Zach, with his coal-black hair and dark inscrutable eyes, had become a recluse, a man who rode alone and didn't seem to need or want a woman in his life.

Thanks to the Fearless Threesome, Falcon was used to escaping the consequences of his folly. Was it any wonder he had been careless and irresponsible with his fortune? Only this time, he didn't think he could ask Zach or Callen to help him out of his trouble. Maybe it was time to grow up at last. Maybe it was time to act like the dependable, reliable, trustworthy person his parents had raised him to be.

"Isn't there something I can do to help Mara and Susannah?" Falcon asked the man sitting across the desk from him.

Aaron chewed on his pencil, a habit that was apparent from the series of teeth marks that already creased the yellow stem. "There is one thing."

Falcon waited, but when Aaron didn't speak he asked, "All right, what is it?"

"You could marry her."

"What?" Falcon leapt up and slammed his palms flat on Aaron's marble-topped desk. He leaned forward intimidatingly. "What purpose would that serve?"

"Thanks to your capable accountant, you have an excellent health-care plan. You see, the insurance company wanted your business for health coverage of employees at the B-Bar. So I was able to negotiate a special clause in the contract that allows you, as the owner, to cover your dependents—even for a preexisting condition—as soon as you acquire them, in this case, by marriage."

"That's incredible."

Aaron smiled. "I thought so myself when I wrote it into the agreement with the insurance company. You can marry Mara Ainsworth and have Susannah's medical expenses one-hundred-percent covered the next day."

"I have to think about this," Falcon said as he rose and headed for the office door. He paused with the doorknob in his hand and turned back to Aaron. "Are you sure that's the only way I can help?"

Aaron shrugged. "You could always sell the B-Bar and give her the proceeds."

Falcon grimaced. "Don't be ridiculous."

"I was being frank," Aaron retorted. "Your choices are limited, Falcon. Let me know what you decide to do."

Falcon left his accountant's office in a daze. He was dealing with a lot of emotions all at once, not the least of which was shame. What would his parents say, especially his mother, when she found out how profligate he had been with her father's bequest to him? And how was he going to face Mara Ainsworth and admit the truth? That he had managed to run through a fortune in five years of dissipated living. What would happen to Mara and Susannah if he couldn't provide her with the funds she had requested?

*You could marry her.*

How could he marry a woman who despised him? A woman who would never forgive him for making her a widow? A woman who shrank from his touch?

Unfortunately he had no choice. And neither did she, when it came right down to it. They would just have to make the best of it. It would be one of those marriages of convenience, where they shared the same name and the same house, but nothing else.

It would be a royal pain in the rear.

But it wouldn't last forever. Just until Susannah was out of deep water. Just until the crisis was over. He could stand being close to Mara for that long without touching.

He didn't linger and let himself come up with excuses why Aaron's suggestion wouldn't work. He jumped into his Porsche and headed for the address on the paper Mara had stuffed in his hand when she had raced away from the B-Bar yesterday.

He found her house on a shady street in an old, quiet neighborhood in Dallas. There were bicycles in the driveways and tire swings in the trees. The houses were two-story wood frame structures with picture windows and big, covered front porches. There was even one house with a white picket fence. It belonged, he discovered, to Mara Ainsworth.

He didn't see a car in the driveway, so he wasn't expecting her to be home. But he knocked anyway.

She opened the door wearing very short cutoff jeans and a Dallas Cowboys T-shirt. She was barefoot. And she wasn't wearing a bra. He knew because her nipples peaked the instant she set eyes on him.

He turned her on, but she hated his guts. It was just plain crazy. He had fought the attraction he felt, knowing it could lead nowhere. But it was clear to him, if not yet to her, that some powerful magnetism still existed between the two of them.

"Hello," he managed.

"Oh! I thought you were my neighbor, Sally. But, of course, you aren't."

Of course he wasn't. He stood there on the porch for a moment, waiting for her to invite him inside. When she didn't, he took a page from her book and stepped inside on his own. He heard the door close behind him.

"Where's Susannah?" he asked when she didn't immediately appear.

"She's still in the hospital."

"Oh."

Falcon looked around with a critical eye, wanting to find something about Mara's home that he could dislike as much as she disliked him. The living room was done in quiet colors and simple Western patterns that were easy on the eye. She had a green thumb, because there were lush plants everywhere, bringing the outdoors inside. Plump pillows decorated the couch, and a cozy, overstuffed chair invited him to sit down.

Only, he knew better than to make himself comfortable. Once she heard what he had to say, she might very well throw him out. He turned to face Mara.

She was leaning against the door in much the same way he had done, but there was nothing relaxed about the pose.

"I didn't bring a check," he said.

She caught her lower lip with her teeth. "You changed your mind about helping us?"

"No, I didn't change my mind," he retorted irritably. "I don't have the money."

She snorted in disbelief. "You mean you choose not to loan it to me."

He began to pace, like a tiger in a cage. "No, I mean exactly what I said. I don't have the money." He paused in front of a natural-rock fireplace and leaned both palms against the mantel with his back to her. "It seems I've already spent most of my fortune. I only have enough left to keep the B-Bar in business."

"I'm sorry," she said.

He whirled, his eyes blazing. "I don't need your pity."

"I don't pity you," she said.

No, it wasn't pity he saw in her eyes. It was disappointment. And disgust. He felt a burning rage deep inside that he should be subjected to all this.

*It wasn't my fault. I wasn't the one who killed Grant Ainsworth. Why should I feel responsible for rescuing Grant's wife and child?*

If not for the situation he found himself in, it wouldn't have been anyone's business but his own whether he squandered his fortune.

"You could have told me all this in a phone call," Mara said. "Why did you bother coming here?"

"Because even though I can't give you the money I promised, there is a way I can help you."

He saw hope blossom bright and beautiful in her eyes. And dreaded the moment of disillusionment when he told her what he had to say.

"If you marry me," he announced, "Susannah will be covered by my insurance the day after we tie the knot."

"What?"

He thought she was going to faint, so he went to her, to help her. He stopped in his tracks when she backed away from him.

"I don't understand," she said.

"I thought I was very clear," he said in a harsh voice. "My insurance policy will cover any dependents of mine, even for a preexisting condition, the day after I acquire them. If you marry me, my insurance will cover Susannah's treatment."

"Marry you?"

"Yes, dammit, marry me! You don't have to sound so appalled at the idea."

"I'm not... appalled. I'm just... surprised."

Mara crossed to the overstuffed chair and sank into it. "I hadn't thought of getting married again."

"Especially not to the likes of me," Falcon finished for her.

Her brow furrowed. "I don't know what to say."

"Say yes."

She sought out his eyes with her own, and he could see the turmoil there. He knew he ought to let her refuse. Then he would be out of it, and the problem would be hers again. But the truth was, he wanted to be the one to rescue her. He wanted to redeem himself in her eyes. He wanted to earn her respect. He wanted a chance to prove he wasn't the good-for-nothing she thought he was.

"It doesn't have to be a real marriage," he said. "We'll have to live together, of course. But that shouldn't be a problem."

"I don't want to leave my house."

"It's just a house," Falcon argued.

"It's more than that," Mara said, eyes flashing indignantly. "It's a place where I belong, where I have friends. I can't give that up, too."

She bit her lip to keep from letting the whole of her tragedy spill out at him—namely, her fear that she might soon lose Susannah, as well.

He saw the tears that filled her eyes, ready to brim over. He knew she was going to reject him again, but he had to make the effort to comfort her anyway. He pulled her up out of the chair and into his arms.

To his amazement, she clutched him around the waist and pressed her forehead against his chest and began to sob. He tightened his arms around her and crooned words of solace. He didn't know how long they stood there, but when she finally stopped crying, one of his hands was tangled in her hair and the other pressed her tightly against him.

His throat felt thick. His chest ached. He would have given anything to be worthy of her. But it was too late. He had lived a profligate, self-indulgent existence. Now, without the other two-thirds of the Fearless Threesome to rescue him, he was finally going to have to face the consequences of his behavior.

He knew when she was herself again, because she stiffened in his arms. She didn't struggle to be free, but he knew that if he didn't let her go soon, she would.

"Marry me," he whispered. "I promise I won't do anything to make you uncomfortable in my home. For Susannah's sake. Marry me."

She heaved a ragged sigh that ended in a sob that she quickly caught with her fist. She lowered her hand and raised her tear-drenched face to his. "All right," she said in a hoarse voice. "I'll marry you."

She took a step backward, and he was forced to release her.

"I'll take care of getting the license," he said. "You'll have to get a blood test—"

"I'll take care of that on my own. When?" she asked.

"As soon as possible, don't you think?"

Her face looked ravaged. Her eyes were red-rimmed. But she faced him without flinching this time. "You tell me when and where, and I'll be there."

"I'll help you move your things—"

"I'll leave the house exactly as it is," she said fiercely. "It's my home, mine and Susannah's. When this travesty of a marriage is over—" she choked back a sob "—when Susannah is *well,* we'll be coming back here to live. Now get out! I can't stand to look at you anymore."

Falcon backed away to the door, unable to take his eyes off her. Mara hated him. And he was going to marry her. He told himself it was a sacrifice that he owed her.

But as he closed her door behind him, he couldn't help feeling regret, and even despair.

How the hell were they going to get through the next year together?

# Three

———

It was her wedding day, and Mara felt trapped. This was not the perfect solution she had been searching for, not at all. But at least she didn't have to leave Dallas. She would find some way to keep Susannah in the same school, and she would be able to keep an eye on her house. But she had paid a high price for those small victories. She had to marry the man responsible for Grant's death.

Falcon had promised her it would be a marriage in name only, but in the same breath he had insisted they live together. She supposed there was some danger the insurance company could refuse to pay if they discovered it was a sham marriage, so it had to look real.

But it was a sham. A farce. A pretense. A mockery. She would be Mrs. Falcon Whitelaw. She would be married to a man she despised, a man so irresponsible he had run through a fortune in five years. She had to live in his house, make his meals, iron his clothes. *Be his wife*.

But she would never forgive him. What he had done was unforgivable. And yet, she owed him something for the help he had given her.

Mara felt torn in half. Because there were other feelings she had for Falcon Whitelaw that had nothing at all to do with hate and scorn. She felt drawn to him in a way that was disturbing, to say the least. She had tried to deceive herself, to say that there was no substance to her attraction to the handsome rogue. But her body made a liar out of her every time she got near him.

So how was she going to survive living in the same house with him, seeing him every day?

"Are you ready?"

Mara was jerked from her thoughts by the words Falcon had murmured in her ear.

"It's time," he said.

"I'm ready." She turned to Falcon. He looked as grim as she felt. "Isn't there anybody you wanted to have here? Some family?" she asked him.

"No. You?"

"No. My parents are gone, and I haven't any brothers or sisters." But she knew Falcon had family. Grant had told her about the Fearless Threesome. Falcon must be missing his brother and sister about now. She wondered how he was going to explain all this to them.

As Falcon listened to the judge reading the words legally binding him to Mara Ainsworth, he was wondering the same thing. How was he going to explain a wife and child to his family? How was he going to explain this slapdash wedding, to which none of them had been invited?

He couldn't tell them the truth. But he didn't want to lie. Better to tell them half the truth. That he had met a very special woman, and that he and Mara hadn't wanted to wait to get married. He would promise to bring his wife to meet the family soon but explain that they had to stay in Dallas for the moment because Mara's daughter was sick and needed treatment at the hospital here. That ought to keep them at bay for a little while.

*Then what?*

He would worry about the future when it got here, Falcon decided. Right now he had his hands full dealing with the present.

He answered "I will" at the proper moment and watched Mara's face as she said the same vow. Her complexion was pale, and she had been chewing on her lower lip so it pouted out a little. He wanted to soothe the hurt. Before the thought got much further than that, the judge was telling him he could kiss the bride.

Falcon put his hands on Mara's shoulders, because he suspected she would retreat if he gave her the chance. He was watching her face as he lowered his mouth toward hers, so he saw the moment her eyelashes fluttered down. Her body was rigid beneath his hands, but her mouth... her mouth was soft and pliant beneath his.

Falcon had kissed a lot of women, but there was no time when he had ever felt like this. It was a reverent meeting of lips, and he cherished Mara, giving himself to her and imploring her to take what he offered.

For a moment, she did.

He felt, as much as heard, her tremulous sigh. She gave herself up to the kiss, her trembling body melting into his, her mouth clinging so sweetly that he thought his heart was going to burst with the joy of it.

Then she jerked away with a cry of distress that she quickly stifled. Her eyes, wide and wounded, stared at him accusingly, as though her surrender was all his fault.

Then he was turning away to smile at the judge— or at least to bare his teeth in a semblance of one— and shake the man's hand and receive congratulations. Falcon didn't risk putting his arm around Mara to lead her from the judge's chambers, but he walked as close behind her as he dared.

The judge knew his father, but had promised to let Falcon break the news of his wedding. Even so, Falcon kept up the facade of wedded bliss until the door was closed behind him, because he didn't want any stories about the real state of his marriage getting back to his family. At least not before he had figured out how to explain things that didn't leave him in such a bad light.

Falcon opened the door of his Porsche and made sure Mara's calf-length ivory dress was inside before he closed it after her. They were on their way now to pick up Susannah, who was well enough to come home from the hospital until her induction therapy began. Funny name for it, Falcon thought, *induction therapy,* but that was what the hospital called chemotherapy used to induce remission. Susannah needed six to twelve weeks of treatment, which was scheduled to begin on Monday. With her condition stabilized, she was being allowed to spend the weekend with her family.

"How have you explained our wedding to Susannah?" he asked Mara.

A flush of color appeared on her ashen cheeks. "I told her we met and liked each other very much, so we decided to get married."

Falcon hit the brakes and almost caused an accident. "You told her *what?*"

"What did you expect me to tell her," Mara retorted. "That I was marrying you to get the money for her treatments? She's an impressionable child. I want to leave her some illusions about life.''

"What's going to happen the first time she sees you cringe when I touch you?" Falcon demanded. "Or didn't you think she was going to notice?" he asked sarcastically.

"I..." Mara hadn't, in fact, thought any further than the wedding. She glared at Falcon. "I suppose I'll have to stop cringing," she announced.

"Great," Falcon muttered. "That's just great. What about our sleeping arrangements? How are you going to explain separate bedrooms to this precocious child of yours?"

"I'll be staying in a room next to Susannah," Mara said. "You'll be the understanding husband who wants me to be near my sick child."

Falcon snorted. "You've thought of everything, haven't you?"

"I wasn't able to think of a way to get out of marrying you!" she snapped.

Falcon slid the car into a parking place at Children's Hospital and cranked off the ignition. He turned to face Mara. "All right," he said, "let's get a few things straight before we go in to see Susannah."

Mara crossed her arms over her chest. "I'm listening."

*Big concession,* Falcon thought. "You're the one who wants Susannah to believe this marriage is real. I'm willing to go along with you."

This time Mara snorted.

Falcon ignored her and continued, "So I think we better set some ground rules. First, no more cringing, flinching or stiffening up like a board when I get near you. Can you handle that?"

Mara nodded curtly.

"Second, no more mudslinging, in either direction. Agreed?"

"That's fine with me."

He took a deep breath. "Third, you're going to have to allow me to show you some signs of affection."

"What? No! Absolutely not!"

"You're not thinking this through," Falcon said. "Won't Susannah be sure to make comparisons between the way you act toward me and the way you acted toward Grant? She'll know right away that there's something wrong if I never kiss you, if I never lay a hand on you."

Falcon watched Mara's face. He could see the struggle going on, the war she was waging. He saw the moment she conceded the battle. Her chin came up pugnaciously, and her hands balled into tight little fists.

"All right," she said through gritted teeth. "We'll do this your way." She turned to face him, eyes bright with unshed tears. "But don't push me, Falcon. Because I won't stand for it!"

There were things she had put up with in her marriage with Grant that she had decided in the year since his death she should never have tolerated. She wasn't going to make the same mistake twice. Better to lay down rules with Falcon now that would protect her later.

Falcon could have wished for more cooperation from Mara. At least she had been forced to put a door in the high walls that kept her separated from him. Falcon felt the first signs of hope he had known since he had agreed to this untenable situation. He would be able to hold Mara, to kiss her. Maybe, as she got to know him better, as he earned her respect, she would allow him to do more.

He would have a year to prove himself. Mara had told him that after Susannah had the chemotherapy treatments, her leukemia had to stay in remission for a year in order for her to be deemed past the first hurdle toward a cure. Mara and Susannah would be with him at least that long. And a year was a long time.

"I won't go beyond what I think is necessary to convince Susannah we have a normal relationship," Falcon said at last. He knew his idea of "necessary" signs of affection and hers were likely poles apart. But he wasn't about to make promises he couldn't keep. "Shall we go inside now and get Susannah?"

Falcon had forgotten how much Susannah looked like her mother. Her face had the same oval shape, the same strong cheekbones and short, straight nose. Her eyes were large and wide-set like Mara's.

But he was shocked at the toll her serious illness had taken on Susannah. It was like seeing Mara pale and thin. His heart went out to the little girl the instant her eyes met his.

"How are you, Susannah?" he asked with a cheerful smile. "Do you remember me?"

Mara was sitting on the bed next to her daughter, and Susannah retreated behind her mother, peeping out at him shyly around Mara's shoulder.

"Your mother has some news for you," Falcon said.

Mara shot him a perturbed look, then smiled down at her daughter. "Yes, sweetheart. Falcon and I got married this morning."

Susannah looked curiously at Falcon. "Are you my daddy now?"

Falcon felt the floor fall out from under him. He obviously hadn't focused on all the responsibilities he was taking on. "I . . . suppose I am."

"Will you buy me a pony?"

"Susannah!" Mara exclaimed. "You shouldn't be asking Mr. Whitelaw to buy you things."

"Why not, if he's my daddy?" Susannah demanded. "Will you buy me a pony?"

Mara looked helplessly at Falcon, who shrugged helplessly back. Then he turned his attention to Susannah.

"Sure I will, pumpkin. What color pony did you want?"

Mara's lips pursed. "You're going to spoil her rotten."

"That's what fathers are for," Falcon replied. "Right, Susannah?" He grinned and tousled the little girl's hair affectionately.

Susannah beamed. "Right."

Falcon stopped what he was doing when it dawned on him Susannah's hair was all going to fall out when the little girl had chemotherapy. He kept the smile on his face for Susannah's sake, but he felt sick inside.

Mara saw Susannah's smile, the first one she had seen in weeks, and forgave Falcon for catering to her daughter. Nevertheless, she couldn't help resenting the fact that Falcon was able to give Susannah something that Grant wouldn't have been able to afford. She and Grant had barely been making ends meet, in fact. But she kept her mouth shut about how she felt. She had promised to curb her tongue for Susannah's sake.

Susannah had to ride a wheelchair downstairs, but the moment they reached the hospital exit, Falcon swept the little girl up into his arms. Mara didn't have time to feel left out, because Falcon slipped his other arm around her waist and pulled her close. A quick, warning glance kept her from pulling free.

Mara was glad she hadn't when Susannah reached out and grabbed her hand, so the three of them were completely connected. "Let's go home, Mommy," the little girl said.

"We're going to my house, if that's all right with you," Falcon said.

Susannah frowned.

"I live on a ranch," Falcon added.

Susannah's face brightened. "Will my pony be able to live with us?"

"Yes, he will."

"Is Mommy coming, too?"

"Wouldn't go without her," Falcon confirmed.

"All right. Let's go," Susannah said.

Mara marveled at how little effort it had taken for Falcon to convince Susannah that his ranch was a better destination than the home she had worked so hard to create for her daughter over the past year. But other than the doll Susannah had grasped tightly in her arms, and Mara herself, her daughter apparently had no attachments to the house in Dallas.

To Mara's amazement, Falcon turned out to be a totally charming companion on the trip to the B-Bar Ranch. He kept Susannah entertained with outrageous stories about himself and his siblings. The Porsche plainly needed to be replaced with a family car. Mara didn't relish confronting Falcon on the issue. Maybe he would realize the problem himself.

Falcon had just finished an anecdote when Susannah sighed and said wistfully, "I wish I had a sister. Can you and Mommy get one for me?"

Mara exchanged a horrified look with Falcon, whose lips twisted in a wry smile.

"That's entirely up to your mother," he said, throwing the ball back into her court.

"Will you, Mommy?"

"It's not quite as simple as buying a pony," Mara said as she sent a cutting glance toward Falcon. "Why don't we wait awhile, until you're well. Then we'll see."

Mara saw Falcon's eyebrow arch at the way she had caviled. But she refused to take away any of Susannah's dreams, no matter how farfetched. Especially since there was no telling how much longer Susannah had to dream dreams.

That awful lump was back in Mara's throat, and she swallowed it down and forced a smile to her face. "Besides, you'll be too busy with your new pony to have time for a little sister right away."

"We're here," Falcon announced.

He unbuckled Susannah's seat belt and lifted her into his arms. "Come on," he said. "I want to show you your new home."

Mara followed, feeling forgotten, and though she wouldn't have admitted it, a little jealous of her daughter. Just when she thought Falcon was going to leave her behind, he stopped and set Susannah on her feet in the arch of the Spanish tiled entryway.

"There's a ritual that has to be observed," he said with a wink to Susannah.

Without warning, he swept Mara off her feet and into his arms. "I have to carry my bride over the threshold."

Susannah laughed. "Falcon picked you up, Mommy."

"He sure did!"

Mara was glad Susannah had bowed to Falcon's request in the car and was calling him by his name. It would have been sad to see Grant displaced so quickly by Falcon in her daughter's affections. But children, thank God, were resilient creatures, and Mara was glad Grant's death hadn't devastated her daughter.

"Can you get the door, Susannah?" Mara asked. "If Falcon stands here too long, he just might get tired and drop me."

Susannah laughed at the idea. "Silly Mommy," she said.

Falcon was surprised to hear the teasing quality in Mara's voice. He was enjoying holding her, and he wished he didn't have to set her down until he got her upstairs to his bed. Only it wasn't his bed anymore. He had ceded it to Mara.

Susannah pushed the door open, and he followed her inside. He managed to plant a quick, searing kiss on Mara's lips before he set her down. She shot him a warning look, but with Susannah present, there wasn't much else she could do. Falcon figured all was fair in love and war, and this marriage was sure to have a good deal of the latter.

"Welcome to your new home, Mrs. Whitelaw," he said.

The stricken look on Mara's face came and went so quickly he might have missed it if he hadn't been watching her so intently. But he did see it. He set his back teeth. So she didn't want his name, either.

Falcon had never really desired anything badly that he couldn't buy with money or have for the asking. Now he was finding out what it was like to want something that was beyond his reach. What he hadn't known about himself until this moment was how hard he was willing to strive to achieve his wants. And, though it irked him to admit it, he wanted Mara to want him with the same aching desire he felt for her.

It might take some time for him to find the right methods to win her over, but he was determined to seek them out. However, he was starting at the bottom of a very tall mountain and he didn't think he was in for an easy climb. Still, when he thought of the rewards to be had at the top, he was willing to take the first step.

If he could only figure out what it was.

Right now he had to concentrate on getting the three of them situated in his house. He took Mara and Susannah upstairs to show them the master bedroom and the guest bedroom next door to it.

"I'm in the bedroom downstairs," he said. "That way we won't get into each other's way."

Mara had moved in her and Susannah's things the previous day and had worried about whether Falcon would take one of the other two upstairs bedrooms. She managed not to sigh aloud in relief that he had relegated himself to the downstairs area.

"We'll join you in a little while," Mara said. "I want to change clothes before I start lunch."

Falcon had been dismissed. He took one last look at his wife and new daughter before heading down the stairs.

They joined him an hour later in the kitchen. Falcon took a moment to admire his wife. She was wearing jeans that molded her hips and long slender legs and a plaid Western blouse that had the first two buttons undone so he saw a hint of her rounded breasts. She had rolled up her sleeves and had tied her hair in a ponytail that made her look like a girl again. He wanted to be the teenage boy that got her alone in the back seat of an old convertible and taught her all about the birds and the bees.

"I would have been glad to fix lunch," Mara said when she saw the table set and food waiting to be served.

"It was my pleasure," Falcon said. "It's just steak and baked potatoes and a salad." He grinned roguishly. "I'm afraid that's my entire repertoire."

Mara sat down in the chair he held out for her and watched with raised brows as he poured decanted red wine into a crystal glass.

"Wine?" she said. "At lunch?"

"It's a late lunch," he quipped. "And we did just get married," he pointed out.

Mara flushed and wasn't sure whether it was chagrin or pleasure she was feeling. Maybe it was both. She could be excused for her confusion. This was, after all, a somewhat muddled situation.

Falcon poured some milk into a wineglass for Susannah. "So you can join in our toast to a happy life," he said.

Mara saw how pleased her daughter was to be included in the grown-up ritual. It appeared Falcon Whitelaw had a knack for pleasing females that she hadn't imagined.

Once they were served and Falcon had seated himself, he raised his glass for the toast he had promised. "To a long and happy life," he said.

Mara stared at him aghast. Such a toast might be appropriate for a newly wedded couple, but with Susannah sitting there, her life in the balance, it seemed particularly cruel. Falcon held his glass aloft, ignoring her wordless censure, demanding that she join him.

At last she did. "To a long and happy life," she echoed, clinking her glass against his and against Susannah's.

"To a long and happy life," her daughter said. Susannah grinned and drank some of her milk. "I'm hungry, Mommy. Let's eat."

That was a good sign. Susannah had been nauseous after the interim treatment she had received, and the doctor had given her a Benadryl injection to help counter the sickness. Apparently it was working.

"I was thinking that you might like to come see the horses in my stable after lunch," Falcon said to Susannah.

"Is my pony there?"

Falcon laughed. "Not yet. But I have a few colts and fillies that you might like to pet."

Susannah was beaming again. *How did he do it?* Mara wondered. Maybe the reason she was unable to make Susannah laugh was because she didn't feel much like laughing herself. So perhaps some good would come of staying with Falcon, after all.

"Do you want to come with us?" Falcon asked as he headed out the back door with Susannah after lunch.

Mara felt anxious letting Susannah out of her sight. But she didn't want to spend any more time with Falcon than she had to.

Misreading her indecision, Falcon said, "I'll take good care of her. I won't let her get hurt."

"Susannah's spent a lot of time around horses. She knows how to act." Her words came out sounding sharp and reproachful, and she wished them back. But it was too late. Falcon frowned and turned his back on her.

"We won't be gone long," he said as he let the screen door slam behind them.

Mara looked around at the mess in the kitchen and realized this was a way she could repay Falcon in part for the service he had rendered when he married her. There was more to be done in the kitchen than simply cleaning up after the meal. Falcon obviously hadn't had a housekeeper in a while. The floor needed scrubbing, and the cabinets were disorganized. There were other things she would be able to do when she had more time: curtains for the windows, flowers on the sill, cleaning the refrigerator and the stove. She would settle now for washing dishes and putting away leftovers.

Mara was just wiping down the front of the refrigerator when Falcon returned with Susannah. He had been gone, she suddenly realized, for most of the afternoon. Where had the time gone? She looked around her and saw a kitchen that sparkled. Her eyes shifted back to Falcon.

Mara sensed from the worried look on his face that something was wrong. Susannah had her head on his shoulder, and her arms were wrapped around his neck.

"I didn't mean to keep Susannah out so long," Falcon said. "She got a little tired. I'll take her upstairs for you."

But his eyes said, *Please don't leave me alone with her.*

In fact, Falcon was terrified. Without warning, Susannah had deflated like a balloon with a pinhole in it. One second she was patting the forehead of a pretty bay filly with four white stockings, the next she was hanging on to the leg of his jeans as though that was all that was holding her upright. Susannah had sagged into his arms when he picked her up, almost like deadweight.

He could feel her erratic breaths against his neck, and she had become unusually quiet. He was even more afraid of what Mara would say about Susannah's condition.

"We didn't do anything strenuous," he found himself saying to Mara. He waited for her to pull down the covers so he could lay Susannah on her bed. "One minute she was fine, and the next minute she was practically asleep on her feet."

"It wasn't anything you did," Mara said. "It's the disease. It saps her strength."

She took off Susannah's tennis shoes and covered her with the sheets and a quilt. The little girl was already asleep.

Mara turned to face Falcon and found herself wanting to smooth the furrow of worry from his brow. "She'll be all right again once she's rested."

When the shadows didn't leave his blue eyes, she reached out a hand to him. "It isn't your fault," she said in a quiet voice. "You didn't do anything wrong."

He seemed to notice suddenly that she was touching him. He stared at her hand, then turned his hand to thread his fingers with hers. "Come downstairs with me," he said. "We need to talk."

Mara felt the calluses on his hand, felt the strength of it and felt all kinds of other things that she had no business feeling. For a moment she resisted his gentle tug. Then she was on her feet and he was leading her downstairs.

He sat on the heavy Mediterranean couch of deep wine leather and dark wood and urged her down beside him. He slipped his arm around her and pulled her close.

Mara nestled her head under Falcon's chin and felt the lickety-split beat of his heart and the grip of his hand on hers. She didn't try to free herself or chastise Falcon for his presumptuousness. She knew he needed comfort, and she needed it too much herself to refuse it to him. They sat there for a long time in silence.

Without fanfare, without warning, dusk fell. The light coming in through the arched windows turned pale yellow and pink and orange. It wouldn't be long before it was full dark. "I thought we were going to talk," Mara said.

"We are," he said. "I just needed this first."

"Me, too," Mara admitted.

"Is she going to die?" Falcon asked.

Mara felt the tears sting her eyes. "No."

Falcon tightened his hold on her. "Is that wishing? Or is that the truth?"

Mara told him everything she knew about acute lymphocytic leukemia. About the six to twelve weeks of chemotherapy to induce remission. About the ninety-percent cure rate for the chemotherapy. About the possibility of relapse, which could happen at any time, and which would require the entire chemotherapy treatment all over again.

"If she makes it for a year without a relapse, there's a good chance she'll be home free."

"And if the chemotherapy doesn't work?"

"There's always a bone-marrow transplant."

"And if that doesn't work?"

Mara tore herself from Falcon's embrace; it was no longer comforting. She rose and turned to face him with her hands on her hips, her feet wide-spread in a fighting stance. "What do you want me to say? That Susannah may die? The possibility exists," she said. "Are you happy now?"

He rose and faced her in an equally belligerent stance. "No, I'm not. How can you stand it, knowing what may happen?"

Suddenly all the fight went out of her. "I don't have much choice," she said, her eyes bleak.

"Mara, I—"

Falcon reached for Mara, to comfort her, but she whirled and ran. He didn't go after her. He wished he hadn't let himself get involved. He wished he had borrowed the money from someone to pay for the treatments Susannah needed. Because he didn't think he could stand by and watch Susannah Ainsworth die. Most of all, he didn't think he could bear to watch Mara suffer if her daughter didn't survive.

It was too late to back out now. He wanted Mara. And he had already given a piece of his soul to Susannah. He was bound to both of them by ties he hadn't even begun to imagine existed before they came into his life.

He would make sure Susannah had the best care possible, no matter what it cost. Even if he had to humble himself before his family to get more money to pay for it.

# Four

———

Falcon had been married for two weeks, during which time Susannah had begun induction therapy in earnest. He made it a point to be at the house whenever Mara returned from the hospital with her daughter. He carried the child up to her bedroom from the van he had recently bought to replace his Porsche, holding her limp form in his arms while Mara arranged the bed. Then he settled her under the covers.

It was getting harder and harder to smile for the little girl. But Falcon forced himself to be cheerful. Mara's face was stark, her eyes bleak and worried.

He didn't think so much solemnity could be good for Susannah.

"How are you feeling?" Falcon asked Susannah. He immediately regretted the words, but to his surprise Susannah lifted a flattened hand and tipped it back and forth like airplane wings.

"So-so," she said.

"Why ask when you know she's feeling sick?" Mara rebuked him.

"There's sick, and then there's sick," Falcon said. "Isn't that so, Susannah?" He brush her bangs away from her forehand and a hank of hair came out in his hand.

He turned stricken eyes to Mara, but found no comfort there. She looked as stunned as he felt.

Falcon sought a way to hide the scrap of hair from Susannah, but she saw it and took it from him, inspecting it carefully.

"My hair is falling out," she said matter-of-factly.

"It appears so," Falcon replied cautiously.

"Dr. Sortino says that's a good sign," she explained to Falcon. "He says that means the medicine is working. I want to get a red hat, like my new friend Patsy wears. Is that okay?"

"That's fine, pumpkin," Falcon said. "Your mom and I will see if we can find one." He started to playfully tug a curl that lay on Susannah's cheek and barely managed to stop himself in time. What if it came away in his hand? Susannah's disappearing tresses didn't seem to worry her, but he was still shaken by his recent experience.

Falcon tucked Susannah in and leaned over to kiss her on the forehead. As he did so he realized he was going to be devastated if chemotherapy didn't stop the disease. He had already started reading about bone-marrow transplants. They were horribly painful, and it was difficult to find donors. And they didn't always effect a cure. The statistics weren't encouraging. He couldn't imagine putting Susannah through it, knowing how much she suffered from the induction therapy.

When he stood up, he realized Mara had already left the room. That wasn't like her. Usually she stayed to read to Susannah after he was gone.

"I wonder what happened to your mom," he said.

"She left a minute ago," Susannah informed him. "She was crying again."

"Again?"

"She doesn't think I know, but I've seen her cry lots of times," Susannah confided. "She thinks I'm going to die. Am I?"

Falcon was startled by such frank speaking. He wanted to reply "Of course not!" But that wouldn't have been honest. On the other hand, did an eight-year-old child deserve to hear an honest evaluation of her chances of survival?

*Mara should be answering these questions,* he thought.

Before he could answer Susannah, she asked, "What is it like to die?"

Falcon grinned ruefully. "You've got me there, pumpkin. I can't answer that. My suggestion is that you concentrate on getting well."

Susannah wrinkled her nose. "You never answered my first question. Am I going to die?"

Falcon didn't care if it was a lie. It was the only answer he was willing to give her. "No, pumpkin. You're going to be fine. But you have to rest and take care of yourself."

Falcon was amazed that Susannah accepted his dictum as truth. She closed her eyes and settled back against her pillow.

"Tell Mommy it's okay if she cries. I understand."

Falcon felt his throat swell with emotion. "I'll do that," he managed to say.

He got out of the room as quickly as he could, closing the door behind him.

He didn't have to search far for Mara. She was standing right there with her back against the wall, her chin on her chest, her arms crossed protectively over her breasts.

"Did you hear?" he asked quietly.

She looked up at him and nodded. Her eyes welled with tears. As he watched, one slid onto her cheek.

"I didn't know what to say," he confessed.

"You said exactly the right thing."

"I lied."

"*It was not a lie!* She's going to live!" Mara said fiercely.

Falcon slipped an arm around her shoulder and led her toward the master bedroom. "Susannah's liable to hear us," he warned.

Mara jerked herself free, and instead of going the rest of the way to her bedroom, headed downstairs. "Let's go where we can talk freely."

Falcon followed after her. It hadn't been an easy two weeks of marriage, but he and Mara had managed to remain civil to each other. He had a feeling their truce was about to end.

Mara marched all the way to the kitchen, where she found a glass and some ice and poured herself some tea. She drank half the glass and wiped her mouth with the back of her hand. "All right, let's get this over with."

"I don't want to fight with you," Falcon said.

Mara was filled with pent-up anxiety. If she didn't release it, she was going to burst. She slammed her tea glass down on the table. "You must be missing all those parties about now," she said. "All that late-night carousing... all those women—"

"Don't start," Falcon warned, grabbing her shoulders and giving her a shake. "I'll accept that you're overwrought because of Susannah's condition. That's no reason to take out your frustration on me."

Mara stared at Falcon, stunned at the accuracy of his statement. Dread and fear crowded her every waking moment, making it impossible to act normally. She shuddered at the thought of how she was behaving toward Falcon. True, she despised his irresponsible, devil-may-care attitudes. But if it hadn't been for his lighthearted teasing, his smiles and cajolery, she didn't think she could have survived the past two weeks. And there were so many more weeks to be endured!

She looked up at Falcon and let him see the remorse she felt. "I'm sorry," she whispered.

Her lips were trembling, her eyes liquid with feeling. Falcon didn't think, he acted on impulse. His mouth slanted across hers, and he thrust his tongue inside, meeting hers in a passionate duel. His hands slid from her shoulders across her breasts, and he heard her moan as he cupped their fullness.

Mara's hands slid around Falcon's waist and up his back, as she sought solace for the ache deep inside. She wanted to disappear inside him, to be absorbed into his being so there was no more Mara and Falcon, only one stronger being, more capable of surviving the awful uncertainty of the future.

"Falcon," she whispered in a ragged voice. "Please. Please."

Falcon picked her up and carried her to his bedroom. He kicked the door closed behind them and captured her mouth as he lowered her to the bed.

"Are you protected?" he asked. There was no sense bringing an innocent child into this convoluted situation. Later, if things worked out... But not now.

"Are you?" he demanded in a voice harsh with the need he was striving to control.

Mara nodded jerkily. "Hurry," she said. "Please hurry." It was a strange thing for a woman to ask a man who was about to make love to her. But Mara didn't want time to think about what she was doing. Nor did she want to give Falcon time to change his mind.

Mara wanted to touch his skin, to feel the warmth, the strength of him. She yanked the snaps free on his shirt and shoved it off his shoulders. She tested bone and sinew with her hands, then tasted with her mouth. She heard the zipper slide down on her jeans and felt Falcon pushing them down along with her panties.

Then she was naked to his touch and his hand was caressing her. His fingers slid inside her, first one and then another. She arched beneath him and bucked a little as the pleasure became too intense to bear. She bit his shoulder, hardly aware of what she was doing, only knowing that she wanted him, needed him. Now.

She reached for him and felt the hard bulge that threatened the seams of his jeans. He groaned as she cupped him in her hand and then stroked up and down. He unsnapped his jeans and shoved them down along with his briefs.

An instant later he was inside her. She moaned deep in her throat as she felt the hot, hard length of him thrust once into the welcoming warmth, then retreat and thrust again.

She lifted her hips in a primitive response to him, then reached for his mouth to mimic with her tongue his intrusion below. She gasped as she felt her body begin to convulse. Her fingernails left crescents on his flanks as she urged him deeper. She wrapped her legs around him and held him captive as he released his seed.

It was over too soon.

Mara felt the tears squeezing between her tightly closed lids. She was panting, trying to catch her breath, and failing. She felt totally enervated. And exultant.

And horrified.

What had she done? She shoved frantically at Falcon's broad shoulders, and he rolled over onto his back. He exhaled a deep sigh of contentment. Mara scrambled to her knees, pulling up her underwear and her jeans, which she realized had caught around her ankles. She searched for her shirt, meanwhile crossing one arm across her breasts.

"Where are you going in such a hurry?" Falcon asked.

"I . . . I have to get out of here," Mara said.

Falcon kicked his jeans the rest of the way off. Mara was appalled to realize that they hadn't even been able to wait long enough to get their clothes off! She chanced a glance at Falcon and was sorry she had looked. He looked smugly satisfied. As well he should be. She had practically fallen on him and dragged him to the ground. What on earth had she been thinking? She had just made love—no, no— she had just *had sex* with a man she despised!

She had been seeking comfort, and he had willingly offered it. The cad. The rogue. The cur.

"Don't bother seeing me out," she snapped, shrugging her way into her shirt.

He laughed.

She glared at him. "What's so funny?"

"You are. You can't pretend nothing happened, Mara."

"Oh yes I can!" She turned and marched out the door. At the last instant she was careful not to slam it. She didn't want to take the chance of waking Susannah.

All the way up the stairs Mara pounded her fist against the banister. "How on earth did I let that happen? I'm an idiot. I have to be out of my mind," she muttered.

But the truth was, she had never had such a devastating sexual experience with a man. She wasn't sure exactly what had happened, but she was terrified that she wouldn't be able to resist Falcon if he offered her a chance to repeat the encounter.

How the mighty had fallen.

It was time she reevaluated her relationship with Falcon Whitelaw. Maybe, if she looked hard enough, she could find enough redeeming features in him to justify a second look at the man.

It had been three long weeks since Falcon had made love to his wife—and he *had* been making love, even if she hadn't. Lately she looked sideways at him every time he got near her, as though she expected him to pounce on her and carry her off to his bedroom again. He wouldn't have minded one bit. But it was as clear as a pane of glass that she would fight him if he made the attempt. So he bided his time, waiting for the moment when she came to him.

Falcon needed to talk to someone about his feelings for Mara. Could he really want a woman this bad who went out of her way to avoid him? Was it asking for heartache to keep hoping she would forgive him—and herself—and work with him to make theirs a real marriage? Falcon had mulled the subject until he was nearly crazy but found no answers. Which was when he decided to approach his brother for advice.

Zach was the person closest to him, the person he had always turned to in the past when he needed a sounding board. He didn't want to leave Mara and Susannah for even the couple of days it would take him to visit his brother at Hawk's Way. So he called Zach and asked him to come to Dallas.

"What's going on?" Zach asked.

"I got married," Falcon confessed.

There was a silence on the other end of the line. "Who's the woman?"

"You don't know her," he said. "She has a daughter who's very ill. There were reasons... Look, I don't want to have to explain all this on the phone. Will you come?"

"I'll be there tonight," Zach said.

Zach piloted his own jet, so airline connections weren't a problem for him. Falcon made arrangements to pick him up at Dallas/Fort Worth International Airport.

Falcon realized he would just as soon not introduce his wife to his brother, or his brother to his wife. So he took Zach to a restaurant in town for dinner.

"Where does your wife think you are tonight?" Zach inquired as he folded the menu and set it beside his plate.

"Mara and I aren't accountable to each other."

Zach's brow arched in disbelief. "That's some marriage you have, baby brother."

"There are ... complications," Falcon conceded.

"And?"

Falcon found it difficult to explain his marriage of convenience to his brother. Especially when Zach interrupted him to say, "I've never heard of such an idiotic reason to get married. You should have come to me for the money. Or gotten it from Dad."

His eyes narrowed and Falcon felt his brother's sharp perusal. "Unless you didn't really marry the woman just to help her out of her financial troubles. Is that it? Are you in love with her?"

Falcon flushed. Trust Zach to put his finger on the pulse of the problem. "I have feelings for her," Falcon conceded. He wasn't going to label them love, although they felt suspiciously like it. But only a fool would admit to love under the circumstance. "Unfortunately she hates my guts," he told Zach.

Zach hissed in a breath of air. "That's too bad. Any hope she'll change her mind?"

Falcon flashed his brother a devil-may-care grin that was tremendously hard-won. "I have some hope of it."

"So why did you call me?" he asked bluntly.

"I guess I wanted someone to tell me I *wasn't* an idiot to marry her," Falcon muttered.

Zach laughed. "Sorry I couldn't oblige you. Look, once the kid is well, you can get a divorce and forget all about the woman."

Falcon's lips flattened. "I don't want to forget about her. And the *kid's* name is Susannah."

"Well, well. Baby brother has grown some sharp teeth. If you feel so strongly, why don't you act on your convictions?"

"And do what?" Falcon demanded.

"Woo her. Win her love. Make it a real marriage."

"How?" Falcon asked in an agonized voice.

Zach took a sip of his whiskey. "I have a suggestion. I don't know if you're going to like it."

"I'm desperate. What have you got in mind?"

"Give her an ultimatum."

"What?"

"Tell her you can't be expected to live like a eunuch for the next year, and if she doesn't want you looking cross-eyed at other women, she can fulfill her marital duties."

Falcon flushed. "I couldn't put her in that position."

"Why not?"

"That wasn't part of the original bargain."

"So what?"

"You can be a ruthless, coldhearted bastard, Zach." He pitied the poor woman who ever fell in love with his brother.

Zach shrugged. "You asked for my advice. I've given it. You're welcome to come up with your own solution to the problem."

Maybe it wasn't fair to demand conjugal relations, Falcon thought, but perhaps he could merely *suggest* they start sleeping together. He knew from their one experience together that he and Mara were completely compatible in bed. It wasn't much on which to base a relationship. But it was a start.

"Thanks for coming, Zach," Falcon said.

"Don't mention it. When am I going to meet this paragon?"

"Not this trip," Falcon said. He didn't think he could stand to have Zach see the way Mara flinched when he got near her. It was one thing to admit to his big brother that he had problems, it was another to allow him to witness them in person. "If Susannah's induction therapy is successful we might be able to come for the family Labor Day picnic."

"I'll count on seeing you there." Zach threw his napkin down on his clean, empty plate. "If we're finished," he said wryly, "I think I'd just as soon fly back to Hawk's Way tonight. I can catch a cab back to the airport. I think you should go home."

Falcon rose and shook his brother's hand. "Goodbye, Zach. I think I'll take you up on that."

It wasn't that he thought Mara would be worried about him. She didn't like him enough to worry about him. But he wanted to be there to say goodnight to Susannah before she went to bed.

"Think about what I said," Zach called to his retreating back.

Hell, Falcon thought, it wasn't likely he was going to be thinking about much else.

# Five

─────

"Is Falcon there?"

Mara tensed at the sultry sound of the female voice on the other end of the line. "Yes, he is," she answered.

"Who's this?" the female asked.

"This is his wife," Mara said with relish.

"Oh. Then I don't suppose he's free to fly to New York this weekend."

"That's entirely up to him," Mara said.

"Oooohh."

Mara could tell she had created confusion at the other end of the line. But really, did she have the right to dictate when and where Falcon went? She was his wife, but it was a marriage in name only. If he wanted to go traipsing off to New York with some sexy southern belle, who was she to say him nay. "I'll get him for you," she said as she set the phone down on the desk in Falcon's office.

She found Falcon in the kitchen with Susannah. "There's a call for you," she said.

Falcon picked up the wall phone extension in the kitchen. Mara stood there listening, her arms crossed defensively over her chest. She knew Falcon must have a lot of old girlfriends, and she wanted to know how he was going to handle this situation.

"Oh, it's you, Felicia." Falcon turned his back on Mara and lowered his voice.

"Yes, I am married," he said. "Over two months ago. It was a very small wedding, Felicia. I didn't even invite my family!" he said in exasperation. "New York? This weekend?" He turned to face Mara, an incredulous look on his face. "My wife has no objection to my going? How do you know that?"

Falcon frowned. "She told you so?"

Mara shrugged with great indifference.

"No, I can't go, Felicia. I have responsibilities here."

Even from across the room Mara could hear the other woman's laughter and see Falcon's embarrassed flush.

"I know that's never stopped me before," Falcon hissed into the phone. "Things have changed since I got myself a family."

"I have a daughter, too," Falcon said. "She's eight. As a matter of fact, we have plans of our own this weekend. We're going shopping for a pony. So, I'm afraid I can't meet you in New York. Have a good time, Felicia. Goodbye."

Falcon slammed the phone down and had rounded on Mara in a fury when he noticed Susannah's wide-eyed interest. "You finish your lunch," he said to the little girl. "I want to talk to your mother in private."

He dragged Mara all the way to his office, which was across the hall from his bedroom, and shut the door with an ominous click behind him. Then he turned to face Mara with his legs spread and his hands fisted on his hips.

"How could you dare to suggest to Felicia that I'd be willing to trot off to New York? I'm a married man!" he snarled. "I take those vows seriously."

"It's a marriage of convenience," Mara corrected. "Plain and simple."

"Have I gone out *once* without you in the two months we've been married?" he demanded. "Well, once," he conceded, recalling his meeting with Zach. "But have I spent even one night away from home?"

"No."

"Then what makes you think I'd be willing to go carousing with another woman in New York? Did you *want* me to go?"

"No," Mara admitted in a small voice. She lifted her chin and said, "I . . . I thought you might need to be with a woman."

"And better anyone else than you," he said in a harsh voice. "Is that it?"

Mara dropped her chin to her chest. "I thought . . ."

"You didn't think!" Falcon accused. "Or you would have realized there isn't any woman I want except you!"

Her head snapped up, and her eyes widened in astonishment.

Falcon let her see the desire he felt for her, let his eyes roam her body voraciously. He should have done what Zach recommended. He should have come right home and demanded his husbandly rights.

But when he had returned from meeting Zach he had found Mara with Susannah in the upstairs bathroom. The little girl had her head bent over the toilet, where it had been for an hour. He had sat down beside Mara, and the two of them had stayed with Susannah until she had finally lain her head down in Mara's lap, exhausted. Falcon had carried Susannah back to bed and told her funny stories about his childhood until she had fallen asleep at last.

He had taken one look at Mara's face, at the terror and exhaustion, and known he couldn't ask anything from her that night. Nor had an opportunity arisen over the succeeding days and weeks. Falcon had faced the fact that his needs would have to wait. It was one of the first truly unselfish acts of his life.

Now he saw that his self-sacrifice had earned him nothing in Mara's eyes. She believed he was capable of abandoning her and Susannah for a weekend on the town.

"You must not think very much of me," he said, his brow furrowed with the distress he felt.

Mara realized now the mistake she had made. And why she had made it. She had heard that other woman's voice on the phone, and she had been jealous of her, and of every woman who had ever enjoyed Falcon's attention. Because she wanted that attention for herself.

Unfortunately, for both her sake and Falcon's, she had been too much of a coward to ask for it. He had not made one move toward her since the night they had made love, had not hinted by so much as a look that he wanted to repeat the experience. Meanwhile, she ached whenever she looked at him. Her body coiled with excitement when he merely touched her hand. She couldn't look him in the face for fear her feelings, which she was certain he didn't return, would be blatantly apparent to him. Obviously she had put him in an awkward position when she sought oblivion in his arms. Obviously he hadn't enjoyed it as much as she had. Obviously he hadn't wanted to repeat the experience.

It was easy to believe that he might have contacted Felicia, or that he might have planned to have Felicia call so Mara would let him go. Now he was telling her that she had been wrong. That he would prefer a weekend with her and Susannah to a weekend with a luscious femme fatale in New York.

"I'm sorry," she said. "I mistook the matter. I'll understand if you want to change your mind about spending time with me and Susannah—"

"Sometimes I could just shake you," Falcon said. He suited word to deed and grabbed her by the shoulders. "I burn for you, woman! Can you understand what that means? I want to be inside you. There isn't a moment when I don't remember what you taste like, what you feel like. I don't want another woman. I want you!"

His mouth slanted over hers, and he told her of his desperate need with his lips and his hands. It took a moment for him to realize that she was crying.

He let her go and stepped back, tunneling all ten fingers through his hair. "Hell, Mara. I'm sorry."

She closed her eyes and pressed the back of her hand over her mouth.

"You don't have to worry about that happening again. I can control myself. I'm not an animal."

He turned on booted heel and left the room, closing the door quietly behind himself.

Mara let out a tremulous sob. "Oh, my God. What have I done? And what am I supposed to do now?" she said to the empty room.

How could she want to make love to the man responsible for Grant's death? How could she let him hold her, love her, when she could not forgive what he had done?

More to the point, why was she finding it so impossible to let go of the anger she felt over Grant's death? It had been more than a year. Her feelings of bubbling hostility should have dissipated by now. But whenever she thought of Grant, feelings of vexation, of frustration and annoyance simmered to the surface. Until she could manage to quell those feelings, she would be better off keeping Falcon at arm's distance. For his sake, as much as hers.

Despite their altercation, Falcon was true to his word. He announced to Mara the next time he saw her, that the trip to the auction to find a pony for Susannah was all planned.

"We'll be getting there just in time to see the ponies auctioned, so Susannah shouldn't get too tired," he said.

"Come on, Mommy!" Susannah said excitedly. "Hurry up and get ready. It's time to go!"

Mara felt her spirits lift when she saw how happy and excited her daughter was. She quickly dressed in a Western blouse, jeans and boots and joined Falcon and Susannah outside.

Falcon was sitting on the edge of a tile fountain that graced the courtyard in back of the house, with Susannah in his lap. As Mara came up behind them she saw that Falcon had given Susannah a penny and was telling her to make a wish and toss the coin into the fountain.

"Will my wish come true?" Susannah asked.

"Who knows?" Falcon said. "This may be a magical fountain."

Susannah squeezed her eyes closed and tossed the penny. It landed with a plop that sent water back up onto her face. She opened her eyes and laughed as Falcon brushed the crystal droplets away with his fingertips.

Mara was moved by his gentleness with the little girl. "I'm ready," she announced. But a moment later she realized she wasn't the least bit ready to deal with the things Falcon made her feel.

She stood frozen as his eyes roamed her body. She felt warm everywhere his eyes touched her. She wanted to surrender to him heart and soul. She gritted her teeth against her wayward feelings.

*Remember Grant,* she admonished herself.

But the hate wouldn't rise the way it had so easily in the past.

*That's because you know who's really to blame for Grant's death, don't you, Mara? And it isn't Falcon Whitelaw. Admit it, Mara. You're to blame!*

*You knew what would happen, and you let Grant go anyway. It's all your fault! Your fault! Your fault!*

"Mara? Is something wrong?"

Falcon's interruption silenced the accusing voice in Mara's head. She pressed a hand to her temple where her pulse pounded. "I'm fine," she said. "Shall we go?"

Falcon gathered Susannah in his arms and walked toward Mara. When he reached her, he slipped an arm around her waist and guided her toward the van. Their hips bumped, and she tried to free herself, but his hold tightened. She was aware of the warmth of his hand at her ribs, of a desire to be alone with him, when he could let that hand ramble at will.

*You're crazy, Mara. You're out of your mind. How can you even think about making love to Falcon Whitelaw? He killed Grant!*

No, *you* killed Grant.

Mara chewed on her lower lip, wishing the awful voice would go away and leave her alone.

Falcon saw the furrow on Mara's brow and wondered what was troubling her now. Maybe he shouldn't have let her know how he felt about her. Maybe she was concerned he would try to take advantage of their situation.

It perturbed him that Mara could think he might take by force what she did not willingly offer him. He had never forced a woman into his bed. Despite Zach's advice, he wasn't about to start now. But he didn't think there was anything he could say that would ease her mind. Every time he opened his mouth he ended up with his foot in it. Better to just let sleeping dogs lie.

At the auction Falcon nodded and tipped his hat to the several ranchers he knew, but he didn't approach them as he would have if Mara and Susannah hadn't been with him. He didn't want to have to explain a year from now about his absent wife and daughter. Instead he concentrated all his attention on finding just the right pony for Susannah.

It was quickly apparent that Susannah wanted a pinto.

"I like the ones with patches," she said.

It was up to him to find an animal she liked that also had both excellent conformation and a good disposition. It wasn't until near the end of the auction that he was satisfied with an animal that Susannah also liked.

"That one!" Susannah breathed with a sigh of awe. "Oh, please, Falcon, that one!"

The pony had a white face, with a black patch that ran across his eyes. Falcon was having trouble deciding if the gelding was black with white patches, or white with black, it was so evenly divided by the two colors.

"I'm going to call him Patches," Susannah announced as she hugged the pony's neck after the auction. "You like that name, don't you, Patches?"

They were approached by one of the ranchers Falcon had seen earlier, Sam Longstreet.

"Howdy, Falcon," the tall, rangy man said, tipping his hat. "Are you going to introduce me to this little lady?"

He said "little lady," but his eyes were on Mara when he spoke, so Falcon knew it wasn't Susannah who had caught his interest.

Sam Longstreet and his father had a cattle ranch that bordered Hawk's Way. Sam was a little older than Falcon, maybe two or three years, but his face had more lines and his body was leaner, toughened by long days spent on the range. His sun-bleached chestnut hair was shaggy and needed a cut, and he hadn't shaved in the past day or so. Sam's boots were worn and his jeans frayed. Falcon wasn't sure whether that was because Sam didn't worry about appearances, or whether it meant hard times for the Longstreet ranch. Sam's father, E.J., had some business dealings with Falcon's father, although Falcon wasn't up on the exact details.

"How are you, Sam?" Falcon said. "I'd like to introduce my wife, Mara, and my daughter, Susannah. Mara, this is Sam Longstreet. Our families have been neighbors for generations."

Sam grinned. "It's a mighty big pleasure to meet you, ma'am. You're a sly one," he said to Falcon. "Haven't heard a peep out of your folks about you getting hitched."

"They don't know."

"I won't breathe a word to them," Sam said. "If that's how you want it."

"It's not a secret," Falcon said. "I just haven't found the right moment to tell them the news."

Sam grinned again. "Can I tell E.J?"

That was sure to put the fat in the fire. Word would get back to his father through E.J. that he had gotten married. "Give me a day to call my folks, then be my guest."

So, the moment of reckoning had come. He would have to tell his parents what he had done, and try to keep them from visiting the newlyweds before he had resolved his relationship with Mara.

Sam turned his attention back to Mara. "How did you hook up with this maverick?" he asked.

Falcon saw the consternation on Mara's face and knew she was trying to decide the best way to explain things to Sam.

"We met through an old friend of mine, a former football teammate at Tech," Falcon said. That was the absolute truth, and so much less than the whole story.

"Makes me wish I'd gone to Tech," Sam said, with an admiring glance at Mara. "Didn't make it to college myself." He turned his attention to Susannah, who was rubbing her own nose against the velvety soft nose of her new pony.

He squatted down so his green eyes would be at a level with her hazel ones. "My name's Sam," he said. "What's yours?"

To Falcon's amazement, Susannah didn't run and hide behind her mother. She answered Sam with a girlish, "My name's Susannah. This is my pony. His name is Patches."

Sam reached out to run a big, work-worn hand along the pony's jaw. "He's a mighty fine-looking pony," Sam agreed.

Susannah was wearing her red hat, but it was plain to anyone who looked closely that she was bald underneath it. Sam wasn't the kind of man to miss a detail like that. He exchanged a surprised look of sympathy with Falcon before he set his hands on his thighs and pushed himself back onto his feet.

He didn't ask questions about Susannah. Things hadn't changed so much in the west that a man could ask another man's business uninvited.

"Guess I'd better be getting along," Sam said. "I've got a new bull to get loaded up, and then I'm headed home."

"Be seeing you," Falcon said.

"Hope so," Sam said with a smile aimed at Mara. "Ma'am." He touched the tip of one callused finger to his battered Stetson, a mark of respect to Falcon's wife.

"What a strange man," Mara said.

"How so?" Falcon asked.

"He looks so…dangerous…and yet his eyes are so…kind. Which is the real Sam Longstreet?" she asked.

Falcon shrugged. "I don't know him very well, even though we lived close. He's older than me or Zach, and his father needed him to work on the ranch, so he never socialized much."

"Will he tell your family about us?"

"He'll tell his father, which is the same thing. But not before tomorrow. Which means I need to call them tonight."

"What do you think they'll say?"

Falcon had a pretty good idea, but he didn't want to burn Mara's tender ears. "They'll be happy for us," he lied.

"Come on," he said. "Let's get this pony home where Susannah can ride him."

But by the time they got home, Susannah's good day had gone bad. She was feeling sick and so tired that she could hardly keep her eyes open. Mara and Falcon put her to bed together with promises that she could ride Patches the moment she was feeling better.

"Are you sure the day wasn't too much for her?" Falcon asked as he and Mara left the room.

"The trip was a wonderful idea. It was only to be expected she would get tired," Mara said. "I don't think she would have missed it for anything," she said in an effort to take the guilty look off Falcon's face.

Falcon allowed himself to be assuaged by Mara's absolution. He didn't want to be responsible for making Susannah any sicker than she already was, and if Mara believed the day hadn't been too taxing for her daughter, he was willing to take her word for it.

"I'd like you with me when I make the call to my parents," Falcon said.

Mara followed him into his office and sat on the bench that ran parallel to his desk. Falcon sat down in the swivel chair in front of the oak rolltop.

"What are you going to tell them?" Mara asked.

"That I met a woman, and we got married."

"Won't they ask questions?"

"Probably."

"How will you explain . . . everything?"

Falcon grinned ruefully. "It depends on what they ask."

"You know what I mean," Mara said. "What will you tell them about *why* we got married?"

Falcon fiddled with his computer keyboard. "I don't know."

"Will you tell them the truth?"

"Not all of it," Falcon said. "They wouldn't understand."

"Why do you need me here?" Mara asked.

"They may want to say hello to you, to offer their best wishes," he said. They would want to do more than that, Falcon feared. They would want to know every last detail about Mara Ainsworth Whitelaw.

He dialed the phone number. It was answered on the second ring. His mother was breathless. She had apparently run to answer the phone. "Hi, Mom," he said.

"Falcon! We've been wondering what you've been up to. You haven't been in touch for *months!*"

"I've been busy," Falcon said.

"Surely not too busy to write or call your parents and reassure them you aren't lying dead in a gully somewhere," Candy Whitelaw chastised. "Now, tell me what prompted this call?"

His mother had never been one to shilly-shally around, Falcon thought. "I wanted to let you and Dad know that I got married."

"You what?" His mother called into the other room, "Garth, pick up the phone in there. It's Falcon. He's gotten married!"

Falcon heard his father's deep voice asking, "When did this happen? Do we know the bride? When are you bringing her here to meet us?"

"Is she there?" his mother asked. "Can we talk to her? What's her name?"

"Her name is Mara Ainsworth. She's standing right here. I'll put her on so you can say hello." Falcon handed the receiver to Mara, who looked at it as though it had grown fangs. At last she took it from him and held it to her ear.

"Hello?" she said tentatively.

"Hello, dear," Candy said. "I'm Falcon's mother. We're so delighted to hear the news. When did you and Falcon meet? When was the wedding? Oh, I'm so sorry we missed it!"

"Hello, Mara," Garth said. "Welcome to the family. When are we going to get to meet you?"

Mara wrinkled her nose at Falcon. She held her hand over the mouthpiece and said, "You rat! They're full of questions I think you should answer."

"It's nice "meeting" you at last, Mr. and Mrs. Whitelaw. I—"

"Call me Candy, please," Falcon's mother said. "And Falcon's father is Garth. Now, tell us everything."

"Thank you, Mrs.—Candy," Mara said. "I don't know where to start."

"Where did you two meet?" Garth asked.

"In downtown Dallas. I was there with my husband and daughter and—"

Mara cut herself off when she heard a gasp on the other end of the line. She looked up at Falcon and saw his eyes were squeezed closed. He was shaking his head in disbelief.

"I'm a widow now," she blurted into the phone.

There was a silence and then a relieved sigh at the other end of the line.

"I'm sorry to hear that," Candy said. "Oh, this is so awkward, isn't it, because if you weren't a widow you wouldn't be married to Falcon, and of course I'm glad Falcon found you, but not under such sad circumstances."

"I feel the same way, Mrs.—Candy," Mara said in a soft voice.

"Tell us about your daughter," Garth said.

"Her name is Susannah, and she's eight years old. She's been very ill lately, but we're hoping she'll be well soon."

"Is there anything we can do?" Candy asked.

"Pray," Mara said in a quiet voice.

"It must be very serious," Candy said. "Are you sure—"

"Susannah has leukemia. She's in treatment right now. We'll know more when the therapy is completed."

Again that silence on the other end of the line, while Falcon's parents digested the newest bomb dropped in their laps.

"Let me speak to Falcon," Garth said.

Mara handed the phone to Falcon. "Your father wants to talk to you."

"Dad?"

"What the hell is going on, Falcon?" Garth demanded in a harsh voice. "What kind of trouble have you gotten yourself into this time?"

"No *trouble*, Dad," Falcon answered in an equally harsh voice. "Mara is a widow and Susannah is sick, it's as simple as that. I'm not asking your approval of my marriage, Dad. I was only offering you the courtesy of telling you about it."

"We want to visit," Candy said.

"No, Mom. That wouldn't be a good idea right now."

"Why the hell not?" Garth said.

"Because I said so!" Falcon retorted, resorting to the words his father had always used to justify every order to his children. "We'll try to be there for the Labor Day picnic." It wasn't much as peace offerings went, but it was all they were going to get. "Goodbye, Mom, Dad."

"Falcon—" Garth roared.

"Falcon—" Candy cried.

Falcon gently hung up the phone. "Well, that's taken care of."

"They didn't sound too happy," Mara ventured.

Falcon tipped Mara's chin up with his forefinger. "It's not their life, it's mine. If I'm happy, it doesn't matter what they think."

"Are you happy?" Mara asked, searching his face for the truth.

His thumb traced her lower lip. It was rosy and plump because she had been chewing on it again. "I'm not sorry I married you, if that's what you're asking."

She lowered her eyes, unable to meet his lambent gaze. But she didn't move away from him. Mara felt rooted to the spot. "You should have told them the truth," she murmured.

"Who knows what the truth is," Falcon said enigmatically.

Mara knew he was going to kiss her. She didn't try to escape the caress. Because she needed it as much as she believed he did. His mouth was gentle on hers, his lips seeking solace, not passion. She kept her mouth pliant under his, giving him the succor, the sustenance he sought.

When the kiss ended, she opened her eyes and was moved by what she saw in his.

He cared for her. He wanted her. And he despaired of having her. It was all there on his face.

Mara wished she could give him ease. But the past intruded and would not be silenced.

It had been easy to blame Falcon for Grant's death, even though she was more at fault than he was. Nevertheless, it was hard to let go of her feelings of rage and hate toward Falcon, however undeserved they were. Grant was still dead, and because of Susannah's illness—which was no one's fault at all—her life had been turned upside down.

*There's a great deal of good to be said about Falcon Whitelaw,* a voice inside her argued. *He's not a bad man, he just had a little growing up to do. He's wonderful with Susannah. And he makes your blood sizzle. Would it be so awful to give him what he wants from you?*

Falcon saw the conflict raging within her. She hated him. He tempted her.

He was the one who stepped back.

"Good night, Mara," he said.

"Good night, Falcon," she replied.

She didn't want him to go. She wanted him to stay.

Afraid she might do or say something she would regret later, Mara whirled and fled the room.

# Six

_____

"**W**here have you been?" Mara demanded.

Falcon was astounded to find Mara waiting for him in the kitchen. She had a cup of coffee sitting in front of her. He could tell it was cold, which meant she had been there awhile. He hadn't come home for supper, unable to face the thought of being near her and knowing he couldn't touch. He hadn't been far away, just in the barn, where he had worked soaping saddles that were in better shape than they had ever been, thanks to his restlessness. Was it possible she had been worried about him?

"I was in the barn," he said. "Working on my saddle."

"I thought something had happened to you. It's so late. You're usually in by dark."

"You *were* worried about me," Falcon murmured. "I'm sorry, Mara. I'll let you know where I am next time."

If anyone had told Falcon three months ago that he would have been willing to be accountable to *anyone,* let alone a woman, he would have slapped his knee at the jest and hurt his ribs laughing.

How the mighty had fallen.

Mara rose and crossed to the sink. "Susannah asked about you," she said, as though to deny her own concern.

"Is she all right?" Falcon asked anxiously.

Mara left the cup in the sink and turned to face Falcon. "The doctor thinks she may be in remission."

Falcon stared at her, stunned. Then he whooped and grabbed her around the waist and swung her in a circle. "This is fantastic!"

Mara held on so he wouldn't drop her. "Let me down."

Falcon set her down, but he kept his hands on her waist. He needed to hold on to someone, or he just might float off into space. "I can't believe this is happening. It's too soon. She's only been in therapy ten weeks."

"I know," she said. "It's...a miracle."

Falcon looked at Mara and wondered why she wasn't more excited. "You said *may* be in remission. Is there something you aren't telling me? When will we know for sure?''

"Dr. Sortino wants to do a spinal tap tomorrow. We'll know as soon as he gets the results from the test.''

"Susannah hates those back-sticks," Falcon said. His hands tightened at Mara's waist. "They hurt.''

"I know," Mara said. "Will you come with us tomorrow?''

It was the first time she had asked him to join her. The first sign at all that she needed him for anything other than his money. "I'll be glad to come with you.''

She smiled for the first time since he had come into the house. "I'm glad you'll be there. Susannah has been asking when you're going to come to the hospital with us.''

"She has?''

Mara stepped back, and Falcon let his hands drop. "She's very attached to you," she said.

"I'm attached to her, too," Falcon said.

"Well, that's what I waited up to tell you. Good night, Falcon.''

"Mara, wait." Falcon didn't want her to leave. He wanted to hold her. He wanted to sleep with her in his arms. He thought of the ultimatum Zach had wanted him to give her—how many weeks ago had that been?—and knew he still couldn't do it. Not now. Not yet. Maybe if—when—they found out

Susannah was in remission he could start making husbandly demands of his wife.

"What is it?" she asked.

"What would you think, if Susannah's feeling well enough, about going to Hawk's Way over Labor Day?"

Mara leaned back against the refrigerator and crossed her arms protectively around her. "Do you really think that's a good idea, for me and Susannah to meet your family?"

"You're my wife," he said. "And Susannah is my daughter."

*Not for much longer.*

The words hung in the silence between them. If Susannah was truly in remission, it would change everything. Mara wouldn't need him anymore. She would be able to move back to her house in Dallas with its covered porch and its white picket fence.

"I want them to meet you Mara. Even . . . even if things don't work out between us. I think you're a very special woman. I've felt that way since the first moment I laid eyes on you."

Mara flushed and shot a quick look at Falcon. "I was a married woman when you first met me," she reminded him.

Falcon's lips flattened, and Mara was sorry she had spoken. She had only meant that he shouldn't have been looking at a married woman that way. She hadn't meant to remind him of the catastrophe that had made her a widow. Falcon turned on his heel, and she knew he would leave the house again if she didn't do something to stop him.

"I've been doing some work in your office," she said as his hand reached the kitchen doorknob.

Falcon turned and glanced at Mara over his shoulder. "What kind of work?"

She gave him a lopsided smile. "Your desk was a little disorganized, and so was your computer filing system."

"You've been working on my computer?" He turned completely around and assumed a pose Mara was coming to recognize as his "I'm King of the Roost and Don't Give Me Any Backtalk" stance, his legs widespread and his hands fisted on his hips.

"I've been organizing," she said.

Falcon raised a skeptical black brow. "Organizing?" Lord help a man when a woman started organizing.

"Come with me, and I'll show you some of what I've done."

Falcon knew an olive branch when he saw one. He willingly reached out to take it. "All right. Lead the way."

Falcon had noticed little improvements around the house since Mara had moved in. Certainly her green thumb was much in evidence. There were potted flowers in the kitchen and trees in planters in the living room.

She had stuck patterned pillows on the leather couch to break up the somber expanse and rearranged nearly every vase into a different arched cubbyhole. The heavy curtains in the living room had been removed so the sunshine filtered in during the day, and gingham curtains had been added for color in the kitchen.

The whole house sparkled with cleanliness. She hadn't been kidding about her ability as a housekeeper. Which should have made him less nervous about her bookkeeping talents, but somehow didn't.

Mara hadn't completely rearranged his office. He could—and would—have complained if she had. She had been more subtle than that, making small changes, a book moved here, a file moved there. Of course, the spurs and halter he had been repairing had been relegated to a worktable in the pantry off the kitchen.

It wasn't until he sat down next to Mara at the computer that he realized what significant changes she had made in his bookkeeping system. She showed him how she had organized his files so he could see which stud had covered which mare, which cows had been inseminated by which bull. Amounts of grain that had been fed, and increase in weight on the hoof, were also calculated for his beef cattle.

"This is incredible! How did you learn to do this?" he asked.

"I told you I grew up at my mother's knee. I spent a lot of time looking over my father's shoulder, too," she said with a cheeky grin.

"I'm impressed. Why haven't you ever gotten a job doing this for some rancher?"

"I don't have a college degree," she admitted. "I had just finished my first year of school when I found out Susannah was sick."

Falcon was thinking she didn't need a degree to do his bookkeeping. But he could see that if something ever happened to him, she might need an education. "You should go back and finish," he said.

"I can't until I know Susannah is well."

"With any luck, we'll get good news tomorrow. I think you should plan to go back this fall, Mara. I can hire someone to take care of Susannah while you're in class."

"I already owe you too much."

"You don't owe me anything," Falcon said. "I've done what I've done because I wanted to do it. I wish you'd get it out of your head that you have to pay me back."

Falcon didn't breathe, he didn't move. On second thought, there was something she could do for him. She had presented him with the perfect opportunity to ask for what he wanted from her without giving her an ultimatum.

"There is something you can do for me," he said.

"What?" Mara asked.

He hesitated, then took the plunge. "I need a woman, Mara. You're my wife. I want to sleep with you."

She hissed out a breath, but didn't say anything right away.

He reached out and caressed her cheek with the back of his hand. Her eyelids slid closed. Her teeth caught her lower lip and began to worry it.

"I want to give you what you want," she said. "I know I owe you—"

Falcon jerked his hand away, and Mara's eyes flashed open. He rose to his feet and towered over her. The muscles in his jaw worked as he gritted his teeth. "If that's the best you can do, forget it."

She leapt to her feet and grabbed his arm to keep him from leaving. "I'm trying! I have needs, too," she admitted in a choked voice. "But I can't forget who you are. Don't you understand? I loved Grant. And because of you, he's dead."

"Grant was a drunk who killed himself in a car wreck!" Falcon snarled.

All the blood left Mara's face. "Who told you Grant was a drunk?"

Falcon stared at her, not sure what had upset her so much.

"Who told you Grant was an alcoholic?" she insisted.

"An alcoholic? Was he?" Falcon asked, dumbfounded.

Mara covered her mouth with her hand. She hadn't ever said the words aloud. Not to anyone. She had lived with Grant, realized he had a weakness, and tried to pretend it didn't exist.

Falcon grabbed her by the arms. "Are you telling me that you've blamed me for Grant's death all this time when you *knew* he had a drinking problem?"

"He didn't have a problem—"

"Tell me the truth!"

"Yes! Yes, I blame you. He was going to AA meetings. He had quit for almost six months before he ran into you."

"Is that why he lost all those jobs?" Falcon asked. "Was he drinking on the job?"

"I don't know," Mara admitted miserably. "He gave different reasons for why he was let go."

"And you never checked?" Facon demanded.

"I trusted him!" she said fiercely. There were tears in her eyes that betrayed the truth. The first time, or maybe the second, Grant had been able to fool her. But by the sixth or seventh time he was fired, she'd had no illusions left.

"How could you love a man like that?" Falcon asked, truly puzzled by her devotion to someone who must have caused her untold pain.

She shrugged helplessly. "He was a good father." *When he wasn't drinking.* "And a good husband." *When he wasn't drunk and chasing other women.*

Mara couldn't meet Falcon's intent stare and lie anymore. To him or to herself. It had been easier to blame Falcon than to admit Grant's weakness. Easier to blame Falcon than to admit her own culpability. Because, when all was said and done, she was responsible for Grant's death.

She had known he had a drinking problem. She should have watched him more closely. She should have gone with him.

Mara knew that sort of thinking was irrational. She had read enough since Grant's death, and learned enough in college psychology and sociology classes she had taken, to understand that Grant was responsible for his own behavior. But she couldn't shake her feelings of guilt. She should have been able to save Grant. And she had failed.

"It wasn't your fault," Falcon said in a quiet voice.

Mara's head jerked up, and she sought Falcon's eyes.

"He was an alcoholic. It was his problem. You aren't to blame."

"How did you know..."

"That you blame yourself?"

She nodded.

"Because I couldn't help thinking there was something I could have done to prevent Grant's death. Maybe if I'd noticed how much he was drinking..." Falcon thrust a hand through his hair. "Maybe if I hadn't left that twenty on the table... Maybe if I had stayed with him and made sure he didn't drive home drunk...."

"That's a lot of 'maybe's,'" Mara said.

"Don't I know it!"

"I feel the same way," Mara admitted. "I was his wife. I should have known better.

"After we left you that day, I begged him to call you up and meet somewhere, anywhere besides a bar. He said it was too late for that. He didn't know where to find you to make other arrangements. And he swore he wouldn't be tempted. He swore he wouldn't drink anything stronger than club soda. He had been sober for months before that night, so I believed him. I should have known he wouldn't be able to resist a drink when it was offered to him, especially since he wanted to keep his alcoholism a secret from you. I should have made arrangements to pick him up."

"What about Grant? Doesn't he deserve some of the blame for what happened?" Falcon asked. "Maybe more than *some*," he amended.

Mara thought of all the ugly things she had said to Falcon, all the accusations she had heaped on his shoulders. "I owe you an apology," she said. "Some of the things I said..."

"Apology accepted," Falcon said.

Mara felt awkward. All her animosity toward Falcon had been based on his irresponsible behavior at the bar that had resulted in Grant's death. Bereft of antagonism, she wasn't sure how to interact with him.

"Can we start over from here?" Falcon asked.

"Can you ever forgive me—"

"Can *you* forgive *me?*"

Mara exhaled a ragged sigh. "I'm so sorry, Falcon. For everything I said. I was horrible."

"You were," Falcon agreed.

When her eyes widened in surprise, his lips curled in a roguish grin.

"Sorry," he said. "I couldn't resist."

"Behave yourself," she chided.

They were teasing each other, Mara realized. It was a start. A very good start.

Mara knew there was one way she could show Falcon he was truly forgiven. He had told her what he wanted from her. And if she was going to be honest, she wanted it, too. She reached out, her hand palm up.

"I'm tired," she said. "Let's go to bed."

Falcon arched a brow, but threaded his fingers through hers. "My room?"

She nodded. She didn't want to take a chance on disturbing Susannah. Or on having to explain to Susannah why she was suddenly sleeping with Falcon.

Mara felt unaccountably shy. "This feels strange," she admitted.

"I know what you mean," Falcon said with a rueful twist of his mouth. "I've been wanting to make love to you for weeks. Ever since—"

"Don't remind me," she said, putting a hand to one rosy cheek. "I was an absolute wanton."

"I didn't have any complaints," Falcon said with a grin. When they got to the living room, he tugged on Mara's hand and she followed him around to the couch. He pulled her into his lap and sat there holding her.

She laid her head on his shoulder and let her hand slide around his waist.

"I've been needing this," Falcon said.

"And not the other?" Mara teased.

"Oh, I want that, too. But it can wait."

Mara felt a pleasant sense of expectation. She had been afraid, when she had agreed to give Falcon what he wanted, that he would rush her into bed. She was glad to see he was willing to take his time. She sighed.

"What was that for?" Falcon asked.

"I was just thinking about how badly I've misjudged you."

"So I'm not an irresponsible ne'er-do-well?"

"You did fritter away your fortune," she said.

Falcon stiffened. There was that. He might not have murdered her husband, but he still was not the sort of solid person she might have chosen for a husband. Especially after the bad experience she'd apparently had with Grant. His arms tightened around her. He had done nothing over the past ten weeks to prove he would be a better husband to her than Grant.

Except he had stopped drinking and carousing and spending money like it was water. That had to count for something. He hadn't missed any of those things, either, Falcon realized. Nothing mattered as much to him as Mara. And Susannah. There had to be a way to convince her they belonged together as a family.

"I hadn't planned ever to marry again," Mara admitted.

He didn't want to hear this.

Falcon pressed a kiss to Mara's nape to distract her and felt her shiver. He kissed his way up her throat to her ear and teased the delicate shell with his tongue.

Her hand slid down to the hard bulge in his jeans. She traced the length of him through the denim with her fingertips. He drew in a breath of air and held it.

"Mara," he whispered in her ear.

"Yes, Falcon."

"Sweetheart, let's go to bed."

She didn't answer with words, just rose and headed for his bedroom, leaving him to follow behind her.

Mara knew she was asking for heartache. The more attached she let herself get to Falcon, the harder it was going to be to leave him when Susannah was well. The truth was, she was terrified of getting involved with another man. Falcon hadn't gotten drunk during the past couple of months, but that didn't mean he wouldn't revert to his former behavior sometime in the future. Grant had been sober for months at a time during their eight-year marriage. She didn't yet trust Falcon not to become another Grant.

There was still the awful uncertainty about whether Susannah would survive. And there were no guarantees Falcon wouldn't be claimed by an accident working on the ranch, or driving in his car. How could she dare make any kind of commitment to another human being who might be taken from her?

But, oh, how she was tempted to throw caution to the winds. The more time she spent with Falcon, the more feelings she had for him. He was funny and generous and gave of himself wholeheartedly. He was compassionate and caring. He was a scintillating lover. Such a man would make some woman a very good husband. He just happened to be hers at the moment.

She knew it had been unfair to expect Falcon to remain celibate during their marriage. She owed him tonight, at least. But she wasn't promising more. She couldn't promise more.

Mara stood at the foot of Falcon's bed feeling awkward, uncertain what to do next. Their previous coupling had been a frenzied thing, more an act of desperation than anything else. She had needed solace and forgetfulness, and Falcon had provided those things in lovemaking that was so passionate it had taken away all thought and left only feeling.

Mara didn't know what to expect now.

Falcon was also aware of how different their joining together was this time. He wanted to show Mara the tenderness he felt, as well as the ardent passion.

"May I undress you?" he asked.

Mara nodded, suddenly shy. Although she didn't know why that should be. He had seen everything before. But she realized, as Falcon slowly undressed her, admiring her with his eyes and his hands and his mouth, that there had been no time before to truly appreciate each other's bodies.

"I want to touch you, too," she told him.

He shook his head. "It would be too distracting. I wouldn't be able to enjoy what I'm doing."

As his mouth closed around a nipple and he suckled, she surrendered to his ministrations. His hands caressed her skin, and the roughness of his callused fingertips raised frissons of sensation wherever they coursed.

Falcon tried to tell Mara with his hands and his mouth how much he adored her, how much she meant to him, how necessary she was to his very life. He wished he was better with words so he could tell her how he felt. Of course the word *love* never entered his head. He couldn't think such thoughts when he knew she hated him. But she had forgiven him. She had no reason to hate him anymore.

Mara was amazed at how her body responded to the touch of Falcon's hands, the feel of his lips on her skin. She experienced things Grant had never made her feel in eight years of marriage. How was she able to find so much pleasure in the arms of another man?

Mara stiffened imperceptibly, but Falcon was sensitive enough to her response to know something had gone wrong. She was no longer giving herself up to his caresses as she had been a moment before.

"Mara?" he murmured in her ear.

She gripped his waist tightly with both hands and for a moment he wasn't sure whether she was going to pull him close or shove him away. Then her arms slid around him.

"Hold me, Falcon," she said. "Make love to me."

"I will, darling. I am."

Falcon meant what he said. He was making love to Mara. But when he had her under him, and when he had brought her to satisfaction, he did not feel like shouting with joy. He felt like crying instead. Because he knew that what he was feeling for her was all one-sided. He had made love to her. She had submitted to having sex with him.

He tried not to let the despair overwhelm him. There was still time to win her love. There was still time for a happy ending.

He was torn, because as much as he wanted Susannah to be well, he knew her recovery heralded the end of his time with Mara. He would have to find a way, and soon, to convince Mara that she couldn't live without him.

Because he knew now he couldn't live without her.

# Seven

—

Over the months he had been forced to stay close to the B-Bar because of his responsibilities toward Mara and Susannah, Falcon had made an astounding discovery.

He liked being a rancher.

His skin had browned in the Texas sunshine, and a fine spray of sun lines edged his blue eyes. His hands had been callused before, but now they were work-hardened. His body had been honed by hard physical labor until he was a creature of muscle and bone and sinew.

He had made hard decisions, and most of them had turned out right. A recent visit to his accountant had confirmed what he already knew. His attention to the details of running the B-Bar was making a difference. Things functioned more smoothly. There was less waste. And the profit margin on the sale of his cattle and horses was higher. To add sugar to the pie, one of the risky investments Aaron had advised him against making had started paying huge dividends.

"If you keep this up, you're going to be rich again," Aaron teased.

Only, it looked like he wasn't going need any of his reacquired wealth to pay medical bills.

Susannah was in remission.

The induction therapy had worked more quickly and efficiently than even Dr. Sortino had hoped. It had only taken ten weeks for Susannah's white blood cells to register normal.

Falcon was amazed at what a difference good health made to Susannah's behavior. She sparkled, she fizzed, she had an absolutely effervescent personality. She was tremendous fun to be with. Falcon teased Susannah that she was so bouncy she was liable to take off some day and go right through the ceiling.

"I don't want to sit still ever again," Susannah said.

"Not even to eat supper?" Falcon had asked.

"Well, maybe for that," she conceded, stuffing a man-sized spoonful of mashed potatoes into her mouth.

When Falcon looked to Mara, to share the humor of the situation, he found her brow furrowed, her eyes dark and despairing. Despite Susannah's good health, Mara didn't appear happy. Falcon dragged her away to the living room after supper to find out what was bothering her. He settled her on the couch and sat down on the coffee table across from her.

"What's wrong?" he asked.

"I want to expect the best, that Susannah is out of deep water," Mara said. "But I can't help dreading the worst, that her good health is a mirage that's going to disappear if I take my eyes off her."

"You have to live for today," Falcon chided.

"I might have expected you to say something like that," Mara snapped.

Falcon flushed. "Once upon a time, I might have deserved that comment," he said. "Not anymore. I'm as anxious as you are to plan for the future." *With you.* "But there's no planning ahead in Susannah's case. She's either going to stay well, or she isn't. There's nothing you, or I, or all the worrying in the world can do to change that."

Mara's eyes were bleak. "You're right," she said. "I know you are. I just can't seem to shake this feeling . . ."

"Then Susannah and I will just have to do it for you." Falcon set out then and there to put a smile on Mara's face. He enlisted Susannah's aid. "Hey, Susannah," he called to the little girl.

Susannah popped up in the living room like a jack-in-the-box. "What is it, Falcon?"

"I say your mom is more ticklish than you are. What do you think?"

"Ticklish?" Mara said warily. "Who said anything about ticklish?"

Falcon grinned and approached her, hands outstretched, ready for serious tickling.

Mara jumped up and ran.

Falcon chased her.

When he caught her, he wrestled her to the floor and hog-tied her with his hands, like she was a newborn calf.

Mara was breathless, she was laughing so hard. "Falcon, stop! I just ate supper."

He leered at her like the villain in a melodrama. "She's all yours, Susannah. Have at her."

Susannah tickled her mother in the ribs and under the arms and behind her ears and on the soles of her feet.

Mara laughed so hard she howled. "Oh, stop," she cried through her giggles. "Oh, please, stop."

"What do you think, Susannah?" Falcon said. "Should we let her up."

"I guess so."

"Of course, this experiment is only half over," Falcon said, perusing Susannah with a speculative eye. "We haven't seen yet how ticklish *you* are."

Susannah screeched, "Help, Mommy!" but Falcon caught her before she had taken two steps and pulled her into his lap, where he began to tickle her mercilessly.

By that time Mara had recovered slightly, and she rescued her daughter. "I think there's someone here who needs a little of his own medicine," she said to Susannah.

"Yeah!" Susannah said as she launched herself against Falcon's chest.

Her attack knocked Falcon onto his back on the floor, and before he could recover, Mara had joined her daughter tickling his ribs.

Falcon was *very* ticklish.

He howled, he begged, he pleaded. "Please, no more!"

He could easily have escaped their attack at any time. He was bigger and stronger than both of them combined. But Falcon didn't want to escape. He loved being tickled by the two women in his life. He loved seeing their smiling faces and their eyes crinkled with laughter. Their chuckles and giggles and guffaws made him feel warm deep inside.

He let them tickle him until they were exhausted, until they fell onto the Navajo rug on either side of him and sighed with happy fatigue. He smoothed his fingers across the prickly crew cut that was all the hair Susannah had grown back so far. His other hand tangled in Mara's silky black tresses. He pulled them close on either side of him and closed his eyes and wished to be this happy the rest of his life.

But it was only a moment in time and not to be captured or held except in memory.

After that night, however, Mara seemed to let go of some of her fear. She didn't offer a smile often, but Falcon treasured every one. As Susannah regained her strength, she and Mara began riding out to meet him when he was working on the range.

The first time it happened, Falcon reached for his shirt and dragged it on over his sweat-slick body. But Mara seemed to find the dark hair in the center of his bronzed chest, and the droplets of moisture that slid down his breastbone, absolutely mesmerizing. So the next time he just left his shirt off and basked in the pleasure of knowing she found pleasure in looking at him.

Not that either one of them would have acknowledged the sexual tension that sparked between them.

Mara was more determined than ever that she and Susannah were going to return to her house in Dallas. It was safer not to get any more involved with Falcon than she already was. The sooner she escaped his home—and the temptation to succumb to his charm—the better. Now that Susannah was in remission, it was just a matter of marking time, to make sure the cure had taken.

On the other hand, Falcon was encouraged by the fact Mara sought him out when he was working—even though she carted Susannah along as a chaperon whenever she visited him.

Today, Mara had brought along a picnic lunch. They headed for the trees at one of the stock ponds and fought the cattle for enough space to settle down on a blanket and eat.

Falcon knew he would never get a better chance to broach a subject that had been on his mind since his parents had asked when they were going to meet Mara and Susannah. After they had eaten, and while they were lazing around on the blanket in the shade, he casually mentioned his family's annual Labor Day picnic.

"Ever since we've been grown and out on our own, it's been a way for us to get together once a year and exchange news. I've never missed one."

"Can we come, too?" Susannah asked.

Falcon blessed the child for her eagerness. "I'd like it if you did," he said. "I know my mom and dad would like to meet you," he said to Susannah.

"They would?" Susannah said, eyes wide. "Why would they want to meet me?"

"Because you're their first granddaughter." Falcon glanced at Mara from the corner of his eye to see how she was reacting to his discussion with Susannah. Her lips were pursed, and she looked thoughtful.

"Can we go, Mommy?" Susannah asked.

"I don't know, sweetheart," Mara hedged.

"Please," Falcon said.

"Please," Susannah said.

"I suppose we can go—"

"Great!" Falcon said, cutting her off and preventing the qualifications he could see were coming.

"Great!" Susannah echoed, straddling Falcon's belly and jumping up and down.

Falcon rolled her off him so she was caught between him and Mara on the blanket. He had turned on his side, so he could see Mara's worried eyes.

"I'm not really your— And Susannah isn't actually your parents'—"

"Don't sweat it," Falcon said with a grin. "They'll love you. And they'll adore Susannah."

"Falcon, are you sure?"

"Do this one thing for me, please, Mara," he said.

"All right, Falcon," she agreed.

But he could see from the look on her face that she was anticipating disaster. He wasn't so sure she might not be right.

Falcon could feel his stomach knotting as they turned onto the road that led to Hawk's Way. The house he had grown up in was as impressive as ever, with its two-story antebellum facade, its railed porches and four towering white columns. The drive up to the house was lined with gorgeous magnolias, while the house itself was draped with majestic, moss-laden live oaks. It wasn't until he had returned home after leaving for the first time that he realized the house had been built more in the architectural style of the deep South than the typical Texas dogtrot home.

"It's beautiful," Mara said. She turned to meet Falcon's gaze and said, "I envy you growing up here."

"It's just a house," Falcon said. But he had a lot of happy memories here.

When they stopped the car in front of the house, they were greeted by an ancient man with long gray braids who was wearing a buckskin vest decorated with feathers and beads. His copper skin was deeply etched with wrinkles.

"Is that a real Indian?" Susannah asked, awed and somewhat intimidated.

"That's Charlie One Horse. He's got a bit of Comanche blood running through his veins. But I promise he's friendly."

Charlie One Horse, the housekeeper who had brought up the Whitelaw kids—Falcon's father and his aunt and uncles—after Falcon's grandfather had died, raised his hand, palm outward, with great solemnity toward Susannah and said, "How."

"Cut it out, Charlie," Falcon said with a grin. "You're scaring my wife and daughter." Falcon was aware of the pride in his voice when he introduced his family to the man who had been like another grandfather to him.

The old man grinned, exposing a missing eyetooth. "Howdy," he said, nodding to Mara. He turned to face Susannah who had retreated behind

Falcon. "Sorry if I scared you, Susannah. My name's Charlie. I've got some chocolate chip cookies in the kitchen that I baked myself."

"You can make cookies?" Susannah said with a startled laugh.

"Best damn—" he caught Falcon's warning look and quickly amended "—darn cookies you ever ate. Come on and I'll let you taste one."

Susannah looked up at Falcon for permission and reassurance, which he gave. "I can vouch for Charlie's cooking."

"Only one, Susannah. You don't want to spoil your supper," Mara admonished as Charlie whisked her daughter away.

She turned to Falcon and asked, "I didn't think she'd go anywhere with a stranger."

"Charlie doesn't allow strangers in the house. Before he's through she'll be wearing feathers in her hair and war paint on her cheeks.

"Shall we go on inside?" Falcon said. "I'll come back for the luggage later."

To Mara's surprise, there was no greeting party waiting for them in the foyer of the house, nor even in the parlor where Falcon led her.

"This is beautiful," she said as she observed the scarred antiques of pine and oak—all polished to a bright shine—in the parlor. An ancient map was framed over the mantel. "Is this Hawk's Way?"

"Uh-huh." Falcon followed her to the stone fireplace so they could look at the map more closely. "It shows all the various borders of Hawk's Way from the time my ancestors settled here more than a hundred years ago until today."

"It's huge," Mara said

"It's not as big as it once was," Falcon said. "When my elder brother, Zach, reached his majority, my father carved off a piece of the place and gave it to him for his own. Zach calls his portion Hawk's Pride." Falcon showed the lines that indicated the borders of Zach's ranch. "You can see there's still plenty left for my father."

Mara took several steps away from Falcon. She had been much too aware of the way his shoulder brushed against her back, aware of the feel of his moist breath on her neck, aware of *him*. "Where is everybody?" she asked.

Falcon grinned sheepishly. "We're hours earlier than I told my folks we'd be here. I wanted to avoid exactly the sort of crowd at the door you were expecting."

Mara smiled gratefully. "Thank you."

"Then you don't mind them not being here to greet you?"

"I'd give anything for a shower and a change of clothes before I have to meet anybody," she said earnestly.

"Your wish is my command." Falcon quickly retrieved Mara's suitcase, then returned and led her up an elegant winding staircase that ended in a hall with a row of doors on either side. "This is where the family usually stays when they come to visit. This will be our room."

Mara stopped in her tracks. "Our room? I thought..." Mara realized she hadn't been thinking at all. She had slept with Falcon in his room at the ranch, even though her clothes had remained upstairs in the room next to Susannah's. Obviously that facade of separation was not going to be maintained under his parents' roof. "We're staying in the same room?"

Falcon looked at Mara from beneath hooded eyes. "I have no intention of telling my parents the true facts of our marriage. They wouldn't understand. There's a king-size bed in this room, which is plenty big enough for both of us to sleep in without running into each other, if that's what you're worried about."

"Wouldn't it be better just to tell them the truth?" Mara asked.

"Why? What purpose would it serve? My mother would be hurt, and my father would be angry and disappointed. I haven't asked much from you, Mara. I'm asking for this."

For a man who didn't ask much, he had asked quite a lot lately. Mara had known there were pitfalls to this trip, she just hadn't known what form they would take. Now she did. Mara gave a gusty sigh. She supposed she should have expected something like this.

"All right," she said. "I'll play along with your charade." Some imp forced her to add, "But I expect you to stay on your own side of the bed."

Falcon grinned. "You can draw a line down the middle, if it'll make you feel any better. Come on in. This room has an adjoining bathroom, with a great shower."

Mara let him show her around the room, which she learned he had shared with Zach when the two boys were growing up. "His ranch is so close, he doesn't stay here overnight anymore," Falcon explained. "So I inherited the room."

"It's mine now," she said with a teasing smile. "Go away and let me get cleaned up."

"Are you sure you want me to leave?" Falcon asked with a lecherous grin, as he let her push him out the door.

"Absolutely," she said as she shut the door in his face.

Mara turned to peruse the room where Falcon had slept as a boy. The head and footboard of the huge bed were oak. There was an antique wardrobe along one wall and a copper-plated dry sink topped by a patterned pitcher and washbowl on another. An overstuffed corduroy chair with a rawhide footstool at its base was angled in the corner with an old brass standing lamp to provide light to read by. A small, round table held a selection of books secured between two bookends which, she was delighted to discover, were two pairs of pewter-dipped baby shoes. Falcon's and Zach's, perhaps?

The large, sheer-curtained window looked out over the front of the house, toward the long, magnolia-lined drive. There was no lawn to speak of. The prairie had been allowed to run wild.

Like the Three Whitelaw Brats, Mara thought.

It had never crossed her mind to consider how her marriage to Falcon would affect his family. Her mother had died when she was fifteen, and her father had been stomped by a bull he was trying to move from one pasture to another only a year after she married Grant. She had no brothers and sisters, no aunts and uncles.

Falcon, she was discovering, had more family than he could shake a stick at. Mother, father, sister and brother, aunt and uncles. That wasn't all. She had discovered on the drive here that he had numerous cousins who would all be arriving shortly.

Mara took a deep breath and let it out. Could she play the loving wife to Falcon in front of his family? She thought of everything Falcon had done for her and Susannah and knew she could. She need only remind herself of the laughter and joy Falcon had brought to a household that would otherwise have been mired in the somber reality of a life-threatening disease. Oh, yes, she could easily play the loving wife for him.

It occurred to Mara to wonder how much of the adoration in her eyes when she looked at Falcon would be an act.

# Eight

———

Mara had just stepped out of the shower and wrapped a towel around herself when the bathroom door opened without a knock.

"Who—"

"Omigosh! I didn't know anyone was in here!"

Mara stared at the young woman frozen in the bathroom doorway. She had wide-set dark brown eyes that danced with mischief and long black hair tied up in a ponytail with a ruffle of bangs across her forehead. She looked about seventeen. But if what Mara suspected was true, this was Falcon's twice-engaged and never-married twenty-eight-year-old sister.

"I'm Callen, Falcon's sister," the young woman confirmed with a welcoming smile. "You must be Mara."

"I am," Mara said.

Mara didn't know where to go from there. Callen didn't look like she was planning to leave anytime soon, and Mara was too modest to continue drying off in front of her.

Mara realized Callen was giving her a very thorough perusal. "Were you looking for something in particular?" she asked archly.

Callen laughed. "I'm afraid I'm too nosy for my own good," she admitted. "You're not at all what I expected."

"Oh?"

"Falcon's women in the past were... different," she said diplomatically.

Mara knew she should leave it at that. But her curiosity was killing her. "How so?"

"You're very pretty, but Falcon always had an eye for truly beautiful women."

Mara swallowed hard. "I see."

"Obviously Falcon found other things to admire in you besides your looks." Her brown eyes twinkled and she said, "You must have a very fine mind."

Mara saw the teasing smile spread on Callen's face and felt the startled laughter spill from her own throat. It was the first genuine, spontaneous laugh she could remember in months and months. "You *are* incorrigible," she said when she could speak again. "I like you, Callen. Now, what was it that brought you in here?"

"Oh. I was looking for a razor to use on my legs."

"In Falcon's bathroom?"

She shrugged impishly. "He keeps a package of disposable razors in here somewhere."

Mara gestured the other woman into the bathroom. "Be my guest. While you're hunting, I'll just dry off and get dressed."

She closed Callen inside the bathroom and quickly toweled herself off and grabbed clean clothes from the suitcase Falcon had left by the bed. She was wearing no more than a bra and underwear when Callen reappeared.

Callen was holding up a blue plastic razor and had a smug look on her face. "See? What did I tell you?"

"That's great." Mara reached for a turquoise squaw skirt and pulled it on, then added a white peasant blouse and a concha belt. Finally she pulled on stockings and added a pair of short leather Western boots. She shoved her hand through her hair in an effort to shake out some of the wetness.

"Do you need a hair dryer?" Callen said.

"Oh, are you still here?"

Callen sat down on the bed. "I was just wondering."

"What?" Mara said resignedly. Evidently Callen wasn't leaving until she was good and ready.

"What do you see in my brother? I mean, what was it about him that made you decide to marry him?"

*His health insurance,* Mara thought. There was no way she was going to tell Callen that. "You are nosy, aren't you?" she said instead.

"Uh-huh. You're avoiding the question."

Mara searched quickly for some attributes that would make Falcon seem good husband material. "He's fun to be with. He's good with my daughter. He's patient. He's—"

"Falcon?" Callen interrupted. "Patient?"

Mara nodded. "Infinitely. He's gentle and—"

"Gentle?" Callen interrupted again.

"Gentle," Mara repeated firmly. "And of course," she said with a look of mischief, "he has a *very* fine mind."

Callen laughed.

Mara watched as Callen's glance slid to the bedroom doorway. "Oh, hi, Falcon. How long have you been there?" she asked.

"Long enough," he said with a grin.

Mara turned beet-red. She fluffed her hair over her face and eyes to hide her embarrassment.

"I can see I'm de trop," Callen said as she looked from Falcon to Mara and back again. "See you at supper tonight, Mara." She gave Falcon a sucker punch in the stomach as she scooted past him. "You too, Falcon."

A moment later she was gone.

Falcon closed the door, shutting himself inside with Mara. "Well, well," he said. "I had no idea I was such a good husband."

"I had to tell her something," Mara said as she flung her hair back off her face. Her eyes flashed dangerously. "I thought you wanted us to appear a happily married couple to your family."

"I did. I do," he said soothingly. "It's all right, Mara. You lied in a good cause."

"I wasn't lying," she said quietly.

"What?"

"You heard me," she said, meeting his gaze. "You are gentle and patient and kinder than Susannah and I have any right to expect."

He noticed she didn't repeat her boast about his "fine mind," which he had easily recognized for the euphemism it was. The proof was in the way her breasts stood peaked beneath her blouse, the way her cheeks flushed, the way her eyes observed him, dilated with passion.

He didn't wait for an invitation. He took the several steps that separated them and pulled her onto her feet. He slid one arm around and cupped her buttocks, pulling her tight against him. The other hand he tangled in her wet hair, drawing her close for his kiss.

He was gentle. Achingly gentle, even though what he wanted to do was ravage her mouth. And she responded, reluctantly at first, and then ardently, so he started to lose control. He thrust against her, letting her feel his need. He was having trouble draw-ing breath, but he didn't want the kiss to end.

There was one sharp knock and the door opened.

"Falcon, I—"

"Dad," Falcon managed to gasp. He kept Mara close, to hide the state of arousal they were both in.

"Doesn't anybody in this house believe in pri-vacy?" Mara muttered with asperity.

Falcon saw the rueful twist of his father's lips. "Sorry for interrupting. Your mother wants to meet Mara. And Susannah is asking where her mother is."

"Is she all right?" Mara asked anxiously, meet-ing her father-in-law's eyes for the first time.

She would have pulled from Falcon's embrace, but he kept her where she was with the slight pres-sure of his hand on her spine.

"She's fine," Garth reassured Mara. He focused on Falcon when he said, "We'll be waiting for you downstairs when you're finished with what you're doing."

Falcon flushed. He felt like a teenager caught necking on the front porch. "We'll be down in a minute, Dad."

When his father closed the door, he released Mara. She closed her eyes and groaned. "I have never been so embarrassed in my entire life. What must your father be thinking?"

"Exactly what we want him to think," Falcon said. "That we're a happily married couple."

"When you kissed me, did you know he was coming up here to get us?" Mara asked.

"Would it matter if I did?" Falcon said.

Mara sighed. "No, I suppose not." She had wanted to believe he found her desirable. But after what Callen had told her about his taste in women, she must be a very poor second choice. However, she had known for a long time she couldn't hold a man's attention for long. Hadn't Grant taught her that lesson? They had been married only six months when he started flirting with other women. It had been all of a year before she saw signs that he had taken another woman to bed.

Mara hissed in a breath of air. She hadn't thought for a long time about that night. About the humiliation she had felt when she had confronted Grant, expecting denial and getting none.

"A man needs a woman now and then," Grant had said.

"And what am I?" she had cried, her heart breaking in two.

"You're my wife," he said. "You don't have to worry about me leaving you, sweetheart. But there are itches I have that you can't scratch."

Mara's face had bleached white at the insult. *She wasn't enough woman for the man in her life.*

She had hidden her shame deep. She had been a good wife and mother, and Grant had praised her for those attributes. And he had come to her bed. But that hadn't stopped his trysts with other women.

She had known the fault was somehow hers, not his. That if she was just more of a woman, he wouldn't be straying from her side.

Suddenly all those feelings of inadequacy came flooding back. All because her relationship with Falcon was changing.

When she had first married Falcon, she hadn't been worried about the issues that had caused such trouble in her marriage with Grant, because nothing about her marriage to Falcon was real. The normal expectations in such a relationship hadn't existed. Now she feared that history was going to repeat itself. Not that she had seen any signs of Falcon flirting, but if her experience with Grant was any guide, it was bound to happen eventually.

Only, it shouldn't matter to her what Falcon did, because their marriage was only a matter of convenience. Even if her feelings toward him were not as nonexistent as she could wish.

"Mara?"

Falcon had noticed Mara's pale features, the tense set of her shoulders, the way she worried her lower lip with her teeth.

"It's going to be all right. My parents won't eat you," he teased. "I promise they're going to like you.

"Even though I'm not like the women you've brought home before?"

"I've never brought a woman here before," Falcon said.

"Oh. But Callen told me about the kind of women you're usually attracted to," Mara said. "I'm not anything like them."

"Callen's too outspoken for her own good."

"I'm glad she told me. At least now I have no illusions about our relationship."

Falcon's eyes narrowed suspiciously. "What does that mean?"

"It means I know I'm not the kind of woman you would have freely chosen for a wife, and that as soon as it's possible, I'm going to release you from this marriage."

"Aw, hell," Falcon said, tunneling all ten fingers into his hair. "Look, Mara, the kind of woman a man carouses with and the kind of woman he marries are two different animals."

"You don't have to tell me that," Mara said quietly. "Grant explained the situation very thoroughly."

"What do you mean?"

Mara lowered her eyes so Falcon couldn't see what she was feeling. "I mean he explained how I was a good wife and mother, but he needed other women for...for his other needs."

"That bastard."

Falcon crossed to Mara and grabbed her by the shoulders and gave her a little shake. "Look at me," he commanded. When she had lifted her lids to reveal dark, wounded blue eyes he said, "I'm not Grant."

"You could be like him," she whispered. "I've seen you drunk. And that woman who called you—"

"Is that what you've been afraid of? That I'll turn out to be an alcoholic like Grant? Or a womanizer? I'm nothing like Grant! Haven't you learned that by now?"

"You drink—"

"A whiskey now and then," he interrupted. "Alcoholism is a *disease*," he told Mara furiously. "And I don't have it!"

"What about Felicia?"

"What about her?"

"Why would she think she could call and invite you for a weekend on the town if you hadn't encouraged her?"

"Felicia was a flirt of mine," he conceded, "*when I was single*. I haven't even looked cross-eyed at another woman since I married you."

"But you must have needs—I haven't— Grant always said—"

"I'm not Grant!" Falcon interrupted in a voice hoarse with rage. "You're the woman I want in my bed, the *only woman!*"

"But—"

"Don't say any more, Mara," he warned. "I'm leaving. Come down when you're ready. I'd give the whole game away if my parents saw us together right now." He turned and marched to the door, closing it with a heavy thunk behind him.

Mara was stunned by Falcon's outburst. Did she dare believe him? But what reason would he have to lie? And if he wasn't lying, what was she going to do about it? Did she dare trust him not to hurt her as Grant had? Did she dare let herself begin to love him?

She had to put such thoughts aside, at least for the moment. There was a job to do. She had to go downstairs and play the role of loving and contented wife for Falcon's family.

It was easier than she had expected it to be.

In the first place, Falcon's mother, Candy, was a dear. Mara could see how the Three Whitelaw Brats had gotten so spoiled. Candy was an indulgent and adoring mother, and she had her husband twisted around her little finger. Mara was amused at the solicitous treatment the tall, rugged cowboy gave his wife.

She had trouble keeping all Falcon's relatives straight. Honey and Jesse Whitelaw were there with Honey's two older boys from a previous marriage, Jack and Jonathan, and their daughter, Tess. Falcon's Aunt Tate was there with her husband, Adam Philips, and their two grown daughters, Victoria and Elizabeth. His uncle Faron Whitelaw and his uncle's wife, Belinda, had come with their two adopted teenage sons, Rock and Drew. It was a boisterous, motley and exceedingly noisy crowd.

Mara's main concern was that Susannah not get tired out. She watched her daughter carefully, but

Susannah basked in all the attention she got from her cousins-by-marriage. Toward the end of the evening, after a supper that culminated in a food fight in the kitchen while the dishes were being washed, Mara separated her daughter from Rock and Drew and started upstairs with her.

"Come back when you've gotten her settled," Falcon's mother said. "We'll be gathered in the parlor in front of the fire."

Mara couldn't find a polite way to refuse. "All right."

Susannah was so keyed up, Mara wasn't sure she would ever get her settled. Her daughter's hazel eyes were feverishly bright and her cheeks were flushed. Mara pressed her hand against Susannah's forehead, fearing the worst.

Susannah shoved it away. "I'm fine, Mommy. Don't worry about me."

Mara forced herself to smile. "That's what mothers do best," she quipped.

Susannah bounced onto the bed and shoved her feet under the covers. "I can't wait until tomorrow," she said. "Drew said he'll take me riding. They have lots of ponies here! Can you believe it?"

"Now, Susannah, I don't know—"

"Please, Mommy. You have to let me go! Everyone's going!"

"I haven't been invited."

"It's just for kids. No grown-ups allowed."

At that moment Falcon stuck his head in the door. Susannah's room was across the hall from theirs, and would eventually be occupied by several other children. "Everything all right in here?"

"Falcon, tell Mommy it's all right for me to go riding tomorrow."

Falcon turned to Mara and solemnly repeated, "It's all right for me to go riding tomorrow."

"Not *you!*" Susannah said with a laugh. *"Me!"*

"Wasn't that what I said?" Falcon asked.

Susannah snorted in disgust. "Mommmmy! I want to go!"

"It really will be safe," Falcon reassured Mara. "The older boys and girls will take care of the younger ones."

Mara didn't have the heart to refuse Susannah. She pursed her lips ruefully. She had no business judging Candy's indulgent behavior toward her children. Look how lenient she was with her daughter!

"All right," Mara conceded. "You can go."

"Yippeee!"

"If you get a good night's sleep," Mara qualified.

Susannah pulled the covers up under her arms. "Turn out the light, Mommy, quick. I'm ready to go to sleep now."

Mara kissed her daughter on the forehead, using the opportunity to reassure herself that Susannah didn't have a fever. To her surprise, Susannah felt a little warm. "Susannah, are you feeling all right?" Mara asked.

"I'm fine, Mommy. Really, truly I am!"

Falcon crossed past Mara and pressed his own kiss to Susannah's brow. "Good night, pumpkin," he said as he turned out the lamp beside the bed.

He had left the door open, and he and Mara headed for the stream of light from the hallway. He closed the door behind them.

"I hope the other kids don't wake her up when they come to bed," Mara said. "She needs her rest."

"I'm sure they'll be quiet," Falcon said.

"As a herd of buffalo," Mara said with a sideways glance at Falcon.

He grinned. "You're probably right, but the only other choice was to put Mara in with us. I thought she would have more fun with the other kids."

And they would have the privacy that a newly wedded couple should want. He didn't mention that to Mara. She had already coped with enough friendly badgering from his family this evening to know he was right.

"How are you holding up?" he asked her as they headed back down the stairs. "My family can be a little overwhelming."

Mara shot him an arch look. "A *little* overwhelming?"

He grinned. "All right. They're a riot looking for a place to happen." He put a hand on the back of her neck and kneaded muscles that were tight with strain.

Mara groaned. "Lord, that feels so good!"

"Want to come back upstairs with me now? I give a killer back rub." And he was dying to give her one.

Mara hesitated, then shook her head. "I promised your mother I'd come back downstairs."

Falcon turned her to face him. He settled both hands on her shoulders and began to massage the tenseness he found there. He had the satisfaction of hearing Mara moan and watched as her eyes drifted closed in pleasure. "She'll understand if we both disappear," he murmured in her ear.

Excitement shivered down Mara's spine at Falcon's invitation. She was tempted! So tempted. She opened her eyes and saw him looking down at her, his eyes hooded, his nostrils flared. She knew what they would end up doing if she followed him up the stairs. In his parents' house. With his whole family waiting for them in the parlor.

"I don't want everyone leering at me tomorrow morning."

"They wouldn't dare—" Falcon grimaced. They would. He and Mara would be teased mercilessly. "You're right," he said, starting her back down the stairs. "Let's go join the multitudes."

Falcon seated Mara on the floor in front of the fire and settled himself behind her. His arms slid around her hips, and he pulled her close. They had arrived just in time to hear Candy finishing the story of how she and Garth had met and fallen in love, complete with fairy-tale ending.

"That's the most outrageous pack of bullsh—"

"Zach!" Candy admonished. "Keep your cynicism to yourself."

"I want to hear the story of how Falcon and Mara met," Callen said.

Mara stiffened. She hadn't expected this. She shot a frightened look over her shoulder at Falcon, who shook his head once, very slightly, to let her know there was no escape. To her relief, he was the one who undertook the task.

"It's really very simple," he said. "I was walking down the street in Dallas when I spied this absolutely stunning woman on the corner."

"You're kidding, right?" Callen challenged.

Falcon shook his head. "That's exactly the way it happened. Only, the next thing I saw was her daughter, and then a man joined her," he recalled.

A hush had fallen on the crowd.

"Who was the man?" Callen asked.

"He was an old friend of mine, a football teammate from Tech," Falcon said. "He was Mara's husband, Grant Ainsworth."

"I remember him," Garth said. "I met him in the locker room after one of your games."

*What happened to him?*

The silence was pregnant. Falcon said very matter-of-factly, "Grant was killed in a car accident. It was a year later before I saw Mara again, but I knew

I couldn't let her walk out of my life again. I asked her to marry me, and she said yes."

"How romantic," Candy said with a sigh. "True love conquers all."

Falcon realized Mara was squeezing his hand so tightly her fingernails were cutting into his skin. He made himself smile at her. "I've been doubly blessed," he continued. "I got a daughter in the bargain."

"And a pretty little minx she is," Charlie One Horse contributed.

"Falcon told us Susannah has been sick," Candy said to Mara. "But she seems so well now."

"She has—had—leukemia. It's in remission."

"Thank God for that," Candy said.

The discussion shifted to Callen, and the fact that for the first time in years she didn't have a man at her side.

"And thank God for that!" Mara heard Garth mutter.

Mara watched Candy put her fingers over his mouth to shut him up and hiss, "Garth! Be good."

The evening wound to a pleasant close, as couples settled back together to watch the fire burn and to drink a glass of whiskey or brandy or some sweet liqueur. No wine drinkers here, Mara thought with an inner smile. But then, this was the frontier, where things were harder, the elements harsher and life was lived to the fullest.

She caught herself yawning and looked quickly to see if anyone had noticed. To her chagrin, Falcon's father was staring right at her.

"Time for bed," he announced.

She started to say, "I'm not tired" and realized she was. Falcon had to haul her to her feet. Her knees felt like jelly.

"Come on sleepyhead," he said. "We've got a big day tomorrow."

"We do?" Mara said. This day had seemed quite big enough.

"Picnic. Football. Frisbee. Croquet. We've got games to play."

Mara snickered softly. "That we have, Mr. Whitelaw. Games no one else even knows about."

Falcon swatted her on the fanny. "Save the cynicism," he said. "I get enough of that when Zach's around."

Mara undressed in the bathroom and put on a thick terry-cloth robe before she ventured into the bedroom. To her relief, Falcon was already under the covers. To her chagrin, his bronzed shoulders were bare.

She narrowed her eyes suspiciously. "Are you wearing anything under those sheets?" she asked.

"Pajama bottoms," he said.

"Oh. Well. That's okay."

"I'll be glad to take them off," he volunteered.

"Thanks, but no thanks." Mara turned off the light before dropping her robe beside the bed and slipping under the covers. She was aware that she wasn't alone in the king-size bed. It seemed to have shrunk. She could hear Falcon breathing, even believed she could feel the heat of his body.

"Good night, Mara."

"Good night, Falcon."

Mara stared at the ceiling, not the least bit tired. Ten minutes later she said, "Falcon? Are you awake?"

"I am now."

"I like your family."

"They like you, too."

Mara shivered. But she wasn't the least bit cold. "Falcon?" she whispered.

"Why are you whispering?" he whispered back.

"I don't know," Mara whispered. "I don't want to wake anyone."

"I'm the only one in here," Falcon said, "and I'm already awake. Is there something you wanted to say to me, Mara?"

Mara heard the irritation in his voice and wondered what had caused it. "I guess not."

Falcon flipped the light on. He sat up and the sheet dropped to his hips. Mara's eyes shot to the expanse of bare flesh he revealed.

"What is it?" he demanded. "I'm awake, and you have my full attention."

"I was just wondering if you'd still be willing to give me that back rub."

"Why didn't you just say so? I'd be glad to."
Falcon scooted over and ordered, "Turn over onto
your stomach."

Mara did as she was told. Falcon quickly strad-
dled her at the waist and his hands came down firm
and sure across her shoulders and began to massage
the sore muscles there.

"How's that?" he asked.

"Mmmm," she murmured.

"How about getting this nightgown out of the
way?" He pulled the thin straps of her silk gown off
her shoulders and shoved the garment down below
her waist, freeing her arms. "There," he said with
satisfaction.

Mara had a sudden realization of what she had
done. What she didn't understand was why she had
done it. She knew where this encounter was heading, and she had to make up her mind quickly
whether she was going to let Falcon make love to
her.

There was no doubt he was ready and willing.

His hands caressed as well as massaged, and as
her languor increased she knew her resistance was
decreasing.

"Falcon?"

"Yes, love?"

Mara shivered again as he murmured the endear-
ment against her ear.

"Would you like a massage when you're finished
doing me?"

Falcon chuckled. "I would love one," he said. "Just as soon as I finish doing you."

She gasped as he slid his hands beneath her and cupped her breasts, teasing the nipples into tight buds with his fingers. "Falcon?" she whispered.

"Why are you whispering again?" he whispered.

"Because I haven't got the breath to talk," she admitted.

For a long time, neither of them said anything. They spoke with their hands, with their mouths and with their eyes.

When Mara drifted to sleep, she was snuggled tightly in Falcon's embrace. She refused to question the right or wrong of what she had done. For now, he was her husband, and he wanted her. And she loved being with him. Maybe she had heard one too many fairy tales this evening.

Tomorrow was soon enough to let reality creep back in.

# Nine

A single rider galloped hell-bent-for-leather toward the Whitelaw mansion. He leapt from his horse before it had even stopped on its haunches and raced toward the crowd gathered under the live oaks in back of the house.

"Falcon!" Drew called. "Falcon!"

"I'm here, Drew," Falcon said, racing toward the teenager. "What's wrong?"

Mara was sitting at a picnic table with several of the other wives. When she heard Drew's cry she jumped up and ran toward him. "What's wrong?" she repeated only a moment after Falcon.

"It's Susannah," Drew said, his eyes huge and worried. "She's hurt. She fell off her horse."

"Oh, no!" Mara cried. "How bad is it?"

Falcon clutched Mara hard around the shoulders to keep her from seizing Drew's shirt and shaking him. "How is she?" he asked Drew.

"I couldn't tell," Drew confessed. "I left her with the others and rode back to get help. She seemed fine when we started out. We asked her if she could lope, and she said yes."

"She's a good rider," Falcon confirmed.

"But she fell off!" Drew said. "We weren't even going very fast."

"I'm sure you weren't," Falcon consoled the inconsolable boy. Falcon gave Mara a push toward his mother's already-outstretched arms and said, "Keep her here."

"I want to go with you!" Mara said fiercely.

"Wait here," Falcon replied, his voice like granite. "I'll bring her back to you. Call the family doctor and make sure he's here when I get back," Falcon told his father.

Garth nodded.

Mara let Candy lead her into the house. To her relief, Falcon's mother didn't ply her with platitudes like, "I'm sure she'll be all right." They sat together in silence in the kitchen, each with a cup of hot coffee in front of her that neither touched.

It seemed ages before Falcon returned. He had Susannah in his arms.

"She wasn't hurt by the fall," he said quickly, before Mara had a chance to be frightened by her daughter's ashen complexion. "At least, not more than a few scratches."

"Then what's wrong with her?" Mara demanded.

Falcon's blue eyes were bleak as a winter day. "She has a fever. And her lymph nodes are swollen."

Mara felt a chill slide down her arms. "No. No!"

"I think she must have fainted. That's why she fell from her horse."

"This can't be happening," Mara pleaded. "Please, God, nooooo!" she wailed.

"What is it?" Candy asked her son.

Falcon's lips were pressed flat to keep them from trembling. He wasn't sure he could speak past the constriction in his throat. "I think the leukemia is back."

Falcon could say one thing for his family, they rallied around in times of trouble. Zach flew the three of them back to Dallas in his private jet, while Callen promised to drive their car home for them. Garth phoned Children's Hospital to tell them to expect Susannah. Candy volunteered to pack their clothes and send them along with Callen.

The rest of Falcon's cousins and aunts and uncles promised to pray.

Falcon only managed to keep Zach from staying with them at the hospital by turning on his brother like a rabid dog. He bared his teeth ferociously. "Leave us be. We can handle this better alone."

What he really meant was *I don't want you to see me fall to pieces.* He felt like he was already in pieces. Mara wasn't in much better shape. He wanted to be alone with her somewhere in a dark place and put his arms around her and lay his head on her shoulder and comfort her and be comforted.

Zach settled a succoring hand on Falcon's shoulder, which was tensed hard as stone. "You don't have to go through this alone."

"Don't stay," Falcon said starkly. His eyes glittered with unshed tears. His throat had a huge lump in it. If his brother was there, if he had someone to lean on, he might break down completely. If he was alone with Mara, he would have to be strong for her. He would be able to stay in control.

Zach tightened his grip momentarily, then let go. "Call us," he said. "We want to know how Susannah is doing."

Falcon nodded. He couldn't manage any more speech.

Zach swept Mara up in a tight embrace, as though to lend her strength, then let her go. "She'll be all right," he whispered in her ear.

Mara whimpered, the sound of a suffering animal. "Thank you, Zach," she grated out. "I needed to hear that."

Even if she knew it wasn't necessarily true.

When they were alone together, neither Mara nor Falcon seemed to be able to reach out to the other. They sat down in chairs next to each other in the hospital waiting room, but they didn't touch.

At long last, Falcon broke the silence. "Even if it is the leukemia back again, that doesn't mean she won't eventually get well," he said, as though to convince himself.

"But she'll have to start all over with those awful treatments," Mara said in a low voice. "She'll be sick again. And lose the hair she was so pleased to be growing back."

Mara reached out a hand, and Falcon grasped it. They clung to each other in a way people do when they know there is strength and fortitude to be found in the other grasp. Mara raised her eyes and met Falcon's steady gaze. It gave her courage to face whatever was to come.

*He isn't like Grant. He's nothing at all like Grant.*

The revelation came to Mara in those few seconds like a star bursting and shedding great light. Grant had never been there for her when she needed him. He had never offered her strength. He had never been a rock to which she could cling in times of trouble.

Falcon hadn't reached for a bottle in times of trouble, nor sought out another woman. He had reached for her. He had come to her.

That wasn't the end of her epiphany.

*Why, I love him,* she marveled. Mara stared at Falcon as though seeing him for the first time. How had he come to mean so much to her? When had she started caring more for his pain than for her own? When had she started wanting him to love her back?

Her thoughts were cut off by the arrival of Dr. Sortino. Mara knew before he said a word that the prognosis was not good. She rose to her feet, still gripping Falcon's hand, and waited to hear what the doctor had to say.

"The leukemia is back."

Four words. Four frightening words.

Mara bit her lip to keep from crying. She pressed her face to Falcon's chest as though to escape what was happening.

There was no escape.

"We've got her stabilized," Dr. Sortino said. "We'll start the therapy again within the next few days. Don't despair," he said. "Children often have a relapse and then recover completely."

Mara lifted her head and stared at him with liquid eyes. "But some don't," she challenged.

"Some don't," he conceded reluctantly. "We'll have to wait and see."

"Can we see her?" Falcon asked.

"You can look in on her. She's sleeping now. The nurse will show you to her room."

He left then, without saying more. But Mara had heard quite enough.

"Hold me," she said to Falcon. "Hold me."

Falcon needed to feel the warmth of Mara in his arms. Because he was cold. So cold.

"She'll be all right," he told Mara. "She has to be."

But when they saw Susannah lying in the hospital bed, her face almost as white as the sheets, neither could manage an optimistic word. They grasped hands and held on.

"Your pony is waiting for you to get well," Falcon whispered to the sleeping girl. "And your mommy needs some more tickling," he said. "And I need you home to bounce around the house," he said in a choked voice.

He turned to Mara, and this time she took him in her arms and comforted him. His powerful body shook with silent sobs that were all the more intense because he fought them, even as they escaped.

Mara reached out a hand and touched her daughter's cheek. "Good night, Susannah," she whispered. Then, to Falcon, "Let's go home."

There was no question of staying in separate bedrooms. Falcon never let go of Mara's hand. He led her to his room and silently undressed her then undressed himself. He laid her on the bed and joined her there, twining their bodies together.

"I need you," he said.

Mara knew what he was asking. She gave herself to him, gave him the comfort and reassurance and love he needed, and took it in return. It was a gentle joining of two bruised souls who sought solace in each other's bodies.

Mara's heart swelled with love, and she gave Falcon a part of herself that she had kept hidden somewhere deep inside for long years—ever since Grant had told her she was not enough woman for him. For Falcon she could be more, was more, because he sought more from her.

Falcon lay beside Mara and realized that he felt far more than physical satisfaction. There had been a difference in their lovemaking this time, subtle but detectable. Mara had held nothing back. She had been lightning and fire in his arms, and he had found himself burning in her embrace. He knew now that what he felt for her was more than lust, or mere affection, or even admiration. He loved her, body and heart and soul.

He wanted to say the words. He needed to say them.

*I love you, Mara. I want to spend my life loving you. I want you to have my children. Susannah needs brothers and sisters to play with. I'll make you both happy. I promise it.*

But he didn't say any of those things.

She was already asleep.


During Susannah's second bout of induction therapy, any discussion of Falcon's and Mara's life together, their future, was held in abeyance. It was as though Susannah was the glue that held them together. Neither was willing to contemplate what form their relationship would take if something should happen and she should disappear from their lives. It might be too painful to remain together as a couple, because each would see in the other's anguished eyes a constant reminder of what they had lost.

In spite of that, their love grew. It happened in small ways, over many days.

They shared duties taking care of Susannah, relieving each other when one had reached the end of his patience with the sick child's petulant whining on the one hand, or was unable to endure another moment of the little girl's tremendous persistence in the face of her debilitating illness on the other.

They spent their nights together making love. Neither spoke the words each privately thought. They told each other of their love in the only way they were allowed. Because there was no question of committing themselves to each other until—unless—Susannah recovered.

Mara made a point of getting up each morning with the sunrise, as Falcon did, and making him breakfast.

"I can do this myself," he said. "I know you're tired."

She traced the shadows under his eyes with a gentle hand. "And you're not?"

"Some sex goddess keeps me up half the night with her demands on my body," he teased.

"Remind the sex goddess you have to work in the morning, and I'm sure she'll leave you alone," Mara replied pertly.

Falcon pulled her into his arms and showered her face with kisses. "I'd rather miss the sleep," he said, snuggling his face against her hair.

Mara felt loved and cherished and appreciated.

"Get going, you've got work to do," she said as she shoved him out the kitchen door.

Sometimes, late at night, after he had made sweet love to Mara and she had fallen asleep, Falcon returned to his office. He wanted Mara to know she would be getting a husband who was financially responsible if she agreed to extend their marriage beyond its current artificial structure. He was planning for the future, something that hadn't interested or concerned him before Mara came into his life.

One night Mara awoke and found herself alone. She sought Falcon out and found him in his office.

"What are you doing here in the middle of the night?" she chided. "You need your sleep."

He was sitting in the swivel chair in front of his desk, and he circled it to face her. Because it had become second nature to find comfort in his arms, she settled herself in his lap and twined her fingers in his hair, pulling his face down to hers for a tender kiss.

"Now," she murmured against lips that were warm and wet against her own, "tell me what's going on. Are we in financial trouble? Do I need to go back to work as a short-order cook?''

"No," he said, perhaps too emphatically. "The whole reason I'm spending time at this desk is to secure our future together in a way that will leave you free to be home with Susannah." *And any other children we have.*

Falcon hesitated, aware he had crossed an invisible line. When Mara gave him no encouragement, he backed up again, into neutral ground. "I'm just making sure the ranch is run well and reinvesting what money I have in less risky ventures."

"You're a man who needs risk in his life," Mara said in a quiet voice.

"Not this kind," Falcon objected.

"Then let me see if I can provide another kind," Mara said, as she bit the lobe of his ear. Her hand slid across his naked chest and down toward the pajama bottoms he wore in case he had to check on Susannah during the night. He was already hard by the time her hand got to him.

"Mara," he warned. "It's nearly dawn. I have to get dressed and go to work in an hour."

"We've got a whole hour? That should be enough time for what I have in mind."

A moment later she was on her back on the floor of his office, and he was inside her. Their loving was stormy and tempestuous, full of risk, and she climaxed twice before he was finished and lowered himself, chest heaving, to the carpet beside her.

Falcon groaned. "I'm sorry, Mara. I didn't mean to be so rough."

She took one look at the love bite she had left on his shoulder and laughed. "I'm sorry, Falcon. I didn't mean to be so rough, either."

Once, during those weeks and months while their lives were on hold, Mara took herself back to the house she had bought because of its location on a quiet, tree-lined street where children played. She was amazed to see it was just an ordinary house. There was nothing particularly special about it. Yet, keeping this home was one of the reasons she had been willing to marry Falcon Whitelaw.

She let herself in and wandered through the house. It felt empty, despite the furnished rooms. She wondered what it was that had made this place seem so much a necessary part of her life. And realized it wasn't the house, but what it had represented. Permanence. A place of belonging where memories could be made.

This house wasn't a home. A home was where people lived and loved. Home was where Falcon and Susannah were. Home was the B-Bar Ranch.

Mara threw herself on the bed in her room and wept. For all the might-have-beens with Grant. What would their life have been like if only...? There, in the house where she had sought the happiness she had been denied in her marriage with

Grant, she let go of the past. Her first love was dead and buried. He no longer had the power to hurt her.

The only question now was whether she had the courage to put aside her past fears and reach out and grasp what she wanted. It meant taking risks. She might be hurt again. She might not live happily ever after. It all came down to a matter of trust.

Did she trust Falcon Whitelaw—who less than a year past had been an irresponsible, carousing, ne'er-do-well—to offer her a future filled with happiness? Or would a lifetime with him be filled with trials and tribulation? Had he merely been on his best behavior for the months they had spent together? Would he revert to form once Susannah was well?

Mara sat herself down on the edge of the bed and dropped her head into her hand. There were no guarantees. She was going to have to take a chance. She was going to have to make up her mind one way or the other. Because she knew that the moment Susannah was out of danger—and she *would* be someday soon—Falcon was going to starting asking questions and demanding answers about their relationship.

And she would have to answer yes or no.

# Ten

---

"Hi, Mom. I'm at the hospital."

"Falcon? What is it? Is it bad news?"

"She's in remission."

"That's wonderful, Falcon!" his mother said. "Oh, I'm so glad for all of you!"

"Tell Dad for me, and Zach and Callen." Falcon didn't think he could handle talking to all of them. He was having trouble keeping his voice steady as it was.

"How's Mara?" Candy asked.

"She's fine."

"When will we see you again?" Candy asked.

"I don't know, Mom. Everything is pretty hectic right now. I'll call you again when things are more settled. Okay? I've got to go now."

"Goodbye, Falcon. Take care of yourself. Give our love to Mara and Susannah."

*When things are more settled.* Falcon wasn't sure how soon that would be. Certainly not until he had an answer from Mara about whether or not she was willing to end their sham marriage and start a real one. Although, since the day of Susannah's relapse, there had been nothing halfway about Falcon's commitment to his wife. Mara had given him hope that she felt the same way he did, but until the words were spoken, nothing was *settled*.

It had taken the full amount of time—Christmas had come and gone—for the induction therapy to work a second time. Even Susannah welcomed the "back-stick" that had resulted in the news that she was in remission again.

"We're going to take things a little slower this time," Mara gently admonished her daughter as they rode home from the hospital. "No more bouncing off the walls."

Falcon winked at the little girl. "You'll have to settle for bouncing on the beds," he teased.

Mara shot Falcon a warning look. She had almost lost Susannah the last time. She wasn't taking any chances with her daughter's health now that she had been given a second lease on life.

Falcon had different ideas about what was appropriate behavior for Susannah's present state of health, and during the next few weeks, the two adults were constantly at loggerheads over what Susannah could and could not do.

"You can't keep Susannah wrapped up in cotton batting," Falcon argued.

"I can, and I will!" Mara retorted.

"She's a little girl. She needs to run and play."

"What if she gets sick again?" Mara said, her heart in throat.

Falcon pulled her into his arms and rocked her back and forth. "We'll make sure she rests, but she has to be allowed to live as normal a life as she can, Mara."

Mara knew Falcon was right. She was being overprotective. "But I'm so scared," she admitted in a small voice.

"I'm here," he said. "I'll watch over you both," he promised.

It was as close to a declaration of love as he had ever come. He wanted to go further. He wanted to say the rest. But Mara stopped him.

"I know you'll take care of us," she said. "But I wonder sometimes if it's fair of me to ask it of you. This isn't what you bargained for when you married me," she reminded him.

"But I—"

Again, she cut him off. "I don't want to think about the future. I want to do what you advised me once before. I want to enjoy today for what it brings and forget about tomorrow. Maybe when I know Susannah is going to get well, I'll think differently. But now . . . now life is too uncertain.''

When she said things like that, how could he talk to her about their future together? But neither could he let what she had said pass without challenging it.

"Do you really mean to put your life on hold for however long it takes Susannah to get well? She won't be truly in the clear unless she stays in remission beyond the five-year mark. *Five years,* Mara. That's a long time.''

"I know," she conceded. "When you put it that way, I know I'm being ridiculous. But I need a little time to start believing there will be a future for us— for me and Susannah.''

He was achingly aware he was not included in her picture of the future.

"A year," she said. "If Susannah stays in remission a year, I'll let myself hope again. But it's too dangerous to believe in the future before then. You do understand, don't you, Falcon?''

He did. All too well. Mara wasn't going to make promises to him or to herself that she wasn't sure she would be able to keep. He wanted to say they could have a life together even if the worst happened, and Susannah died. But he discovered he couldn't voice even the possibility that the world might lose a free spirit like Susannah. She had become as dear to him as though she were his own flesh and blood.

\* \* \*

To anyone watching from the outside, they appeared a perfectly normal, happy family over the months of winter that led into spring. In fact, Susannah quickly got well enough to misbehave. That created a whole new set of problems for Mara and Falcon. They were no longer merely caretakers for a youthful invalid, they were parents trying to raise a responsible, honest and self-sufficient child.

Falcon found himself sympathizing with what his own parents must have gone through with him and his siblings. Susannah had gotten used to being waited on and catered to during her illness. The first time Falcon insisted she pick up her damp towel and put it back on the bathroom rack, she responded as the spoiled child she had become.

"You do it," she said.

Falcon wasn't sure what to do next, but he wasn't about to let an eight-year-old order him around. "Pick it up, Susannah. Otherwise, you can go to your room and spend the rest of the morning thinking about ways you can help do your share in this family."

"You're not my father," Susannah shouted back. "You can't tell me what to do!"

Falcon stood stunned, appalled at the child's apparent dismissal of the role he had played in her life over the past nine months. Surely no real father could have been more kind or considerate, more loving or caring during her illness. But children, he was learning, can have short, selfish memories.

"Susannah Ainsworth! You apologize to Falcon this instant!"

Mara had overheard the entire conversation and was appalled at her daughter's devilish behavior. "You will pick up that towel and hang it back on the rack. Then you can go to your room and stay there the rest of the morning!"

"I'm sorry, Falcon," Susannah said in a petulant voice. Then she turned to her mother. "If I've picked up the towel," Susannah reasoned as she sullenly hung the damp towel on the rack, "why do I still have to go to my room?"

"Because you were rude and disobedient," Mara said.

"Why do I have to do what Falcon says?" Susannah complained. "He's not my real father."

Mara looked quickly at Falcon's face, which had hardened like stone, then back to her daughter. She was the one who had forced Falcon to remain on the fringes of her and Susannah's life. She was the one who wanted everything on hold until she was good and ready to move forward. She had created this situation, and the time had come for her to resolve it.

"Falcon *is* your father in every way that matters," Mara said. "He has the right to tell you what to do. And you have the duty to obey him and to treat him with respect."

Susannah turned wide, hazel eyes on Falcon. "Are you really going to be my real father?" she asked, her tone more curious now than belligerent. "Forever and ever?"

Falcon shot one desperate look at Mara, wanting to be able to say yes, and knowing that he hadn't the right.

Mara knew she had to make a decision. "Yes, he is," she answered for Falcon. It was easy, she realized, so easy to say yes to a lifetime with Falcon.

Their glances caught and clung for a moment. Mara almost gasped at the powerful emotions she saw in Falcon's eyes. She knew then she had done the right thing. She was committed to this man. For better or worse. For richer—and he was beginning to spend money like Croesus again—or poorer. In sickness—and there might be more of it for Susannah—and in health. It only remained for the words to be spoken between them.

Only, now that she had taken a step off the edge of a treacherous cliff, Mara was terrified that Falcon wouldn't be there to catch her.

"All right, you can be my father," Susannah said in the way children have of accepting momentous occasions with aplomb. "I'm sorry, Falcon," she said, this time with more contrition in her voice. She crossed to him and put her arms around his waist and said, "Actually, I'm glad you're going to be my father for real and always. I guess I sorta like you a lot." Then she looked up at him with an innocent, angelic face and said, "Do I still have to go to my room?"

Falcon swept the little girl into his arms and gave her a tremendous hug. "God, I love you, Susannah. I'm so glad you're my daughter for real and always." Then he set her on her feet and said, "And yes, you still have to go to your room."

Susannah grimaced. "All right, but if I stay in my room this morning, can we go riding this afternoon?"

Falcon shook his head at her persistence. He sent a questioning look to Mara as if to say, "All right?" When she nodded, he said to Susannah. "Sure. You use the morning to think, and we'll go riding this afternoon."

"Yippee!" Susannah said as she hopped, skipped and bounced away.

In an exaggerated motion, Falcon wiped his brow with his sleeve. "I have great respect for my parents when I see what they coped with from the other side of the fence."

"It isn't easy knowing the right thing to do or say," Mara conceded.

"Did you mean it, Mara? That I'll be Susannah's father for now and forever?"

Mara flushed. "Yes," she said in a whisper. "If you want to be."

"If I want to be? How can you even ask? I *love* Susannah." It would only take another breath to say *And I love you.*

Mara never gave him the chance. "I've got a lot to do this morning if I want to be free to ride with you and Susannah this afternoon," she said.

She backed up a few steps, then turned and almost ran for his office. She was like a skittish filly that had walked up to his hand to take the sugar he held out to her, but at the last moment had taken fright and run. Like the filly, he knew she would be back. Because once a creature had developed a taste for sugar, it was an irresistible lure.

It wouldn't be a bad thing to wait a little while and give his jumbled feelings time to sort themselves out. And give Mara time to realize that he would be there, waiting with his hand outstretched, whenever she was ready to move forward in their relationship.

At least the suspended animation in which they had lived for the past nine months was coming to an end. But Falcon wasn't taking anything for granted. He wanted the words spoken. He wanted things decided once and for all. And if he moved slowly and carefully enough, there was just the chance she would come to him today.

Just before lunchtime, Susannah came running into the kitchen. "Can we go riding now?" she asked. "Patches needs some exercise."

"What do you say, Mara?" Falcon asked. "Shall we go riding now, or after lunch?"

Mara finished wrapping the last of the sandwiches she had been preparing. "I've put together a picnic to take to the stock pond," Mara said. "But mind you, no racing!"

Falcon and Susannah raced the last few hundred yards to the stock pond, with Mara flying close behind.

"Whew! I have to admit that was exhilarating," Mara said with a laugh as she slid off her horse.

"I'm hungry," Susannah said. "Can we eat lunch now?"

"Sure. Untie the blanket from behind your saddle and I'll get the food." Mara began untying the saddlebags on her horse.

Falcon quickly relieved her. "I'll do this. You can help Susannah spread out the blanket."

All of them ate like they were never going to see food again. Replete, they settled back lazily on the blanket and watched the shapes on the ground made by the broken shadows of the leaves.

In a very short while, Mara and Falcon were treated to the sight of Susannah sound asleep on the blanket between them.

"She seems to tire so easily," Mara said as she chewed worriedly on her lower lip.

"Most kids her age take a nap, don't they? Or would if their parents could get them to slow down long enough. She's fine, Mara. Try not to worry so much."

"I do try!" Mara said. She rose from the blanket and walked a few steps away, where they wouldn't disturb Susannah's slumber.

When Falcon came up behind her and circled her waist, she leaned her head back against his shoulder. This felt good. This felt right. She wanted to stay married to Falcon. She wanted them to be husband and wife. But was that fair to him? What if she had trapped him by the things she had said this morning. What if he didn't want to stay with her and Susannah after all? She had to know the truth.

"I took advantage of the situation this morning," she said. "If you want out of this marriage, all you have to do is say so."

"Oh?"

Mara couldn't tell from that one quiet word whether Falcon was relieved or infuriated by what she said. But his hands had tightened uncomfortably around her.

"I can't breathe," she protested.

His hold loosened, but he didn't let her go. Neither did he speak. Maybe he did want out.

She continued, "When Susannah asked if you were going to be her father forever and ever, I said you would. But we've never talked about forever, Falcon. I made the choice for you. I know that's unfair, and if you want to be free of us, of both of us—"

He whirled her around and clutched her tightly at the waist. "Look at me, Mara."

But she couldn't. She was afraid.

He caught her chin between his fingers and forced it upward. He tightened his grasp and demanded, "Look at me."

He waited until she looked up at him before speaking again. His eyes were narrowed, his gaze fierce. A muscle worked in his jaw. This was not a weak man. This was not a man who would let her fall from a cliff. He would be there to catch her.

"I want to be Susannah's father," he said in a harsh, grating voice. "Very much."

"That means you'll also be stuck with me," Mara said with a breezy laugh that somehow got caught in her throat.

Falcon let go of Mara's chin and caught her by the shoulders. "I love you, Mara. I want you to be my wife, forever and ever."

Mara's heart soared when she heard Falcon's declaration of love. But she had to make sure he knew what he was getting into. "Are you *sure?*"

There was a silence that sent Mara's heart to her throat.

Falcon was shaken by Mara's third attempt to set him free. Didn't she hear what he was saying? Didn't she realize how much he loved her? There was only one thing that could possibly change his mind about staying married to her, and that was if she didn't want him. He needed to know that Mara loved him. He needed to hear the words. But he didn't dare ask her outright. What if she said no?

For the first and most important time in his life, Falcon found himself at a loss for words with a woman. "Mara, do you— Is there a chance that— Is it possible—"

"What are you trying to say, Falcon?"

From the blanket behind them a little voice piped up, "Falcon wants to know if you love him, Mommy."

"What?"

Both adults shot startled looks at the little girl, who was lying on her stomach with her head perched on her hands and her legs waving in the air.

"I thought you were asleep," Mara said.

"Well, I'm not," Susannah replied. "Do you love him, Mommy?" she demanded.

Mara flushed, and Falcon feared the worst. He tried to get the words past a constricted throat, tried to offer her the divorce she so obviously wanted. Fortunately he was too distressed to speak.

Because the next words out of Mara's mouth were, "Yes, Susannah, I love him very much."

Mara and Falcon exchanged glances that shouted hosanna and hallelujah, before Falcon pulled Mara into his arms for a possessive kiss. A moment later, Susannah was tugging on his shirt, demanding to be included in the family embrace.

"Love me too, Daddy," she said. "Me, too."

"You too, Susannah," Falcon assured the little girl. "I'll love you and your mommy both, forever and ever."

Falcon met Mara's eyes and they spoke without words. They might not have forever with Susannah. There were no guarantees of long life and happiness. But whatever time they had together, they silently vowed to live to the fullest.

"Let's go home," Falcon said. "I want to make love to my wife," he whispered in her ear.

"Yes," Mara replied in a soft voice. "Let's take our daughter and go home."

*     *     *     *     *

Dear Readers,

You can watch the sparks fly when Callen Whitelaw clashes with Sam Longstreet in *The Headstrong Bride,* book two of the Children of Hawk's Way series.

Coming in December from Silhouette Desire!

Happy trails,

Joan Johnston

Dark secrets, dangerous desire...

# Lovers
## DARK AND DANGEROUS

Three spine-tingling tales from the dark side
of love.

This October, enter the world of shadowy
romance as Silhouette presents the third in their
annual tradition of thrilling love stories and
chilling story lines. Written by three of
Silhouette's top names:

### LINDSAY McKENNA
### LEE KARR
### RACHEL LEE

Haunting a store near you this October.

## MILLION DOLLAR SWEEPSTAKES (III)

No purchase necessary. To enter, follow the directions published. Method of entry may vary. For eligibility, entries must be received no later than March 31, 1996. No liability is assumed for printing errors, lost, late or misdirected entries. Odds of winning are determined by the number of eligible entries distributed and received. Prizewinners will be determined no later than June 30, 1996.

Sweepstakes open to residents of the U.S. (except Puerto Rico), Canada, Europe and Taiwan who are 18 years of age or older. All applicable laws and regulations apply. Sweepstakes offer void wherever prohibited by law. Values of all prizes are in U.S. currency. This sweepstakes is presented by Torstar Corp., its subsidiaries and affiliates, in conjunction with book, merchandise and/or product offerings. For a copy of the Official Rules send a self-addressed, stamped envelope (WA residents need not affix return postage) to: MILLION DOLLAR SWEEPSTAKES (III) Rules, P.O. Box 4573, Blair, NE 68009, USA.

## EXTRA BONUS PRIZE DRAWING

No purchase necessary. The Extra Bonus Prize will be awarded in a random drawing to be conducted no later than 5/30/96 from among all entries received. To qualify, entries must be received by 3/31/96 and comply with published directions. Drawing open to residents of the U.S. (except Puerto Rico), Canada, Europe and Taiwan who are 18 years of age or older. All applicable laws and regulations apply; offer void wherever prohibited by law. Odds of winning are dependent upon number of eligibile entries received. Prize is valued in U.S. currency. The offer is presented by Torstar Corp., its subsidiaries and affiliates in conjunction with book, merchandise and/or product offering. For a copy of the Official Rules governing this sweepstakes, send a self-addressed, stamped envelope (WA residents need not affix return postage) to: Extra Bonus Prize Drawing Rules, P.O. Box 4590, Blair, NE 68009, USA.

SWP-S994

## SILHOUETTE®

## *Desire*®

## Big Bad WOLFE

### WOLFE WANTING
### by Joan Hohl

Don't miss *Wolfe Wanting*, Book 3 of Joan Hohl's
seductively sexy BIG BAD WOLFE series, coming your
way in October...only from Silhouette Desire.

As sergeant for the Pennsylvania State Police
Department, Royce Wolfe was just doing his job—
protecting a violent-crime victim, making sure she
was safe. But he deserved a slap in the face for what
he was thinking about the sexy woman. He wanted
her—bad. But a Big *Bad* Wolfe was the last thing
Megan Delaney needed....

SDJH3

*Premiere*

The stars are out in October at Silhouette! Read captivating love stories by talented *new* authors— in their very first Silhouette appearance.

*Sizzle* with Susan Crosby's
**THE MATING GAME**—Desire #888
...when Iain Mackenzie and Kani Warner are forced to spend their days—and *nights*—together in *very* close tropical quarters!

*Explore* the passion in Sandra Moore's
**HIGH COUNTRY COWBOY**—Special Edition #918
...where Jake Valiteros tries to control the demons that haunt him—along with a stubborn woman as wild as the Wyoming wind.

*Cherish* the emotion in Kia Cochrane's
**MARRIED BY A THREAD**—Intimate Moments #600
...as Dusty McKay tries to recapture the love he once shared with his wife, Tori.

*Exhilarate* in the power of Christie Clark's
**TWO HEARTS TOO LATE**—Romance #1041
...as Kirby Anne Gordon and Carl Tannon fight for custody of a small child...and battle their growing attraction!

*Shiver* with Val Daniels'
**BETWEEN DUSK AND DAWN**—Shadows #42
...when a mysterious stranger claims to want to save Jonna Sanders from a serial killer.

Catch the classics of tomorrow—*premiering* today—
**Only from**

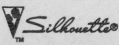

*Silhouette*®

TM

PREM94

## SILHOUETTE® Desire®

### ANNETTE BROADRICK'S SONS OF TEXAS SERIES CONTINUES

Available in October from Silhouette Desire, TEMPTATION TEXAS STYLE! (SD #883) is the latest addition to Annette Broadrick's series about the Callaway family.

Roughed-up rodeo cowboy Tony Callaway thought women were nothing but trouble—but once this lonesome cowboy took one look into Christina O'Reilly's sultry green eyes, he was sure to change his mind!

Don't miss Tony Callaway's story in TEMPTATION TEXAS STYLE! by Annette Broadrick, Desire's MAN OF THE MONTH for October.

**He's one of the SONS OF TEXAS and ready to ride into your heart!**

SDAB

## SILHOUETTE... Where Passion Lives

Don't miss these Silhouette favorites by some of our most
distinguished authors! And now you can receive a discount by
ordering two or more titles!

| | | | |
|---|---|---|---|
| SD#05750 | BLUE SKY GUY by Carole Buck | $2.89 | ☐ |
| SD#05820 | KEEGAN'S HUNT by Dixie Browning | $2.99 | ☐ |
| SD#05833 | PRIVATE REASONS by Justine Davis | $2.99 | ☐ |
| IM#07536 | BEYOND ALL REASON by Judith Duncan | $3.50 | ☐ |
| IM#07544 | MIDNIGHT MAN by Barbara Faith | $3.50 | ☐ |
| IM#07547 | A WANTED MAN by Kathleen Creighton | $3.50 | ☐ |
| SSE#09761 | THE OLDER MAN by Laurey Bright | $3.39 | ☐ |
| SSE#09809 | MAN OF THE FAMILY by Andrea Edwards | $3.39 | ☐ |
| SSE#09867 | WHEN STARS COLLIDE by Patricia Coughlin | $3.50 | ☐ |
| SR#08849 | EVERY NIGHT AT EIGHT by Marion Smith Collins | $2.59 | ☐ |
| SR#08897 | WAKE UP LITTLE SUSIE by Pepper Adams | $2.69 | ☐ |
| SR#08941 | SOMETHING OLD by Toni Collins | $2.75 | ☐ |

(limited quantities available on certain titles)

| | |
|---|---|
| **TOTAL AMOUNT** | $_____ |
| **DEDUCT: 10% DISCOUNT FOR 2+ BOOKS** | $_____ |
| **POSTAGE & HANDLING** | $_____ |
| ($1.00 for one book, 50¢ for each additional) | |
| **APPLICABLE TAXES*** | $_____ |
| **TOTAL PAYABLE** | $_____ |
| (check or money order—please do not send cash) | |

To order, complete this form and send it, along with a check or money order
for the total above, payable to Silhouette Books, to: **in the U.S.:** 3010 Walden
Avenue, P.O. Box 9077, Buffalo, NY 14269-9077; **in Canada:** P.O. Box 636,
Fort Erie, Ontario, L2A 5X3.

Name:_____

Address:_____ City:_____

State/Prov.:_____ Zip/Postal Code:_____

*New York residents remit applicable sales taxes.
Canadian residents remit applicable GST and provincial taxes.

SBACK-SN

*Silhouette*®